SONGBIRD

SONGBIRD
BOOK ONE

SARAH WILLIAMS

Serenade Publishing

www.serenadepublishing.com

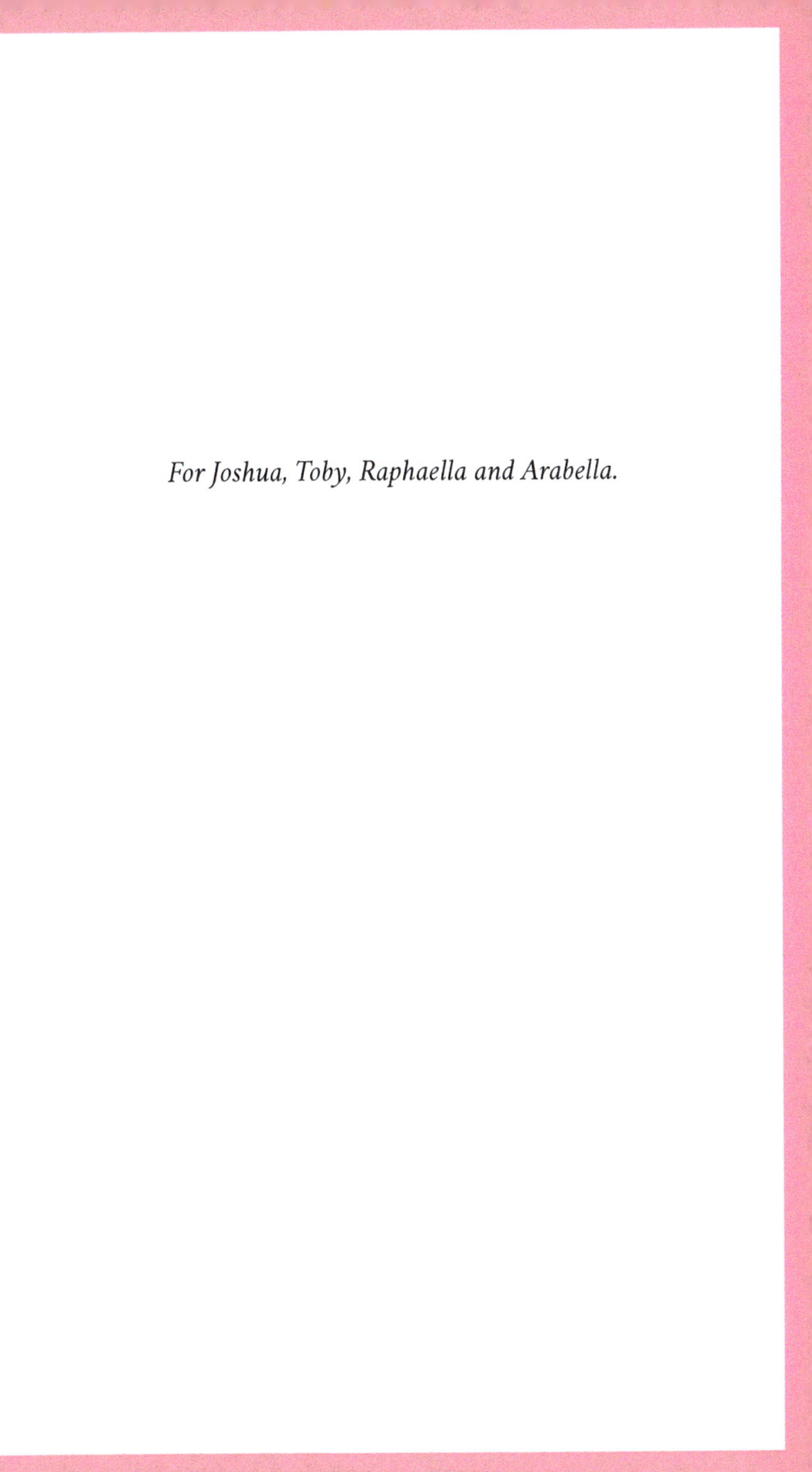

For Joshua, Toby, Raphaella and Arabella.

CHAPTER ONE

ayleigh

IT'S HAUNTING how vividly memories of a traumatic incident can cling to your mind, like shards of broken glass piercing and cutting with every recollection. The smallest details stick like glue, cloying at your sanity and dragging you back into the horror all over again.

As I look through the window at the road ahead, I notice the moon is only a sliver in the night sky. The stars twinkle as clouds pass by.

My parents gave me the secondhand car as a gift for getting my license, and I love everything about it: the way it smells of roses from the cardboard scent which swings from the rearview mirror. I even love the tears in the fabric seats. But mostly, I love the freedom it gives me. The freedom it gives our happy trio.

Chase has his driver's license too, but he has to borrow his mom's car if he wants to drive anywhere, so the two of us, and my little sister, Harper, would take mine for drives around town and to the music store. Sweetgum Valley wasn't a big town, but we kept ourselves busy.

But this is the longest adventure we have gone on. There was a battle of the bands competition in a town two hours away from Sweetgum Valley and after auditioning, we had secured a place in the competition. So this morning, Chase had packed his guitar in the trunk of my sedan, Harper had taken her spot in the backseat, and I had driven us along the winding roads to the festival.

"That was the best night of my life!" thirteen-year-old Harper exclaims behind me on the way home. "Can I keep this in my room?"

I glance at her in the mirror. In the darkened cab I can only make out her silhouette, but I can imagine her fondly stroking the golden trophy we had won for coming first place in our category, her long blonde hair frizzy in the humid night air and her mascara smudged from where she had rubbed her tired eyes.

"I think we should take turns," Chase says from the passenger seat. I can see him more clearly in the light coming from the dash. He reaches across and lays his hand on my thigh. It sends heat flooding through my body. I love when Chase touches me, even innocently like this. I wonder if this is how it will always feel like to be touched by the person you are madly in love with.

"It's finally happening, guys. With this award we can do bigger events than just the ones at the school and around town. We could even record a demo and send it to record labels." I say, my mind buzzing with possibilities. Singing is my passion, and the way our trio sounds, with Chase on guitar and Harper on backup vocals, I know we can achieve the ambitious dreams I've had since the first time I'd sung along to Faith Hill on the radio. Excitement and adrenaline courses through my veins as I imagine playing to sell-out arenas all over the world. We are going to be famous—I just know it.

I force myself to focus on the road. It is so dark and just a sliver of moonlight lights the empty road. We are heading downhill after climbing up the steep mountain's incline. We are nearly home, and I am looking forward to collapsing in my bed and having a big sleep-in tomorrow morning.

A new song starts playing on the radio. It's familiar guitar riff filling the car.

"Oh, I love this song!" Harper exclaims, as her arm brushes past me. "I can't reach."

I hear her unclick her seatbelt, then reach through the gap in our seats to turn up the volume on the radio.

Harper stays perched in the space between us. Her face fills the rearview mirror, and I see her bopping her head as she sings the lyrics. Chase's deep baritone harmonizes and I sway my shoulders in time with the music.

Harper reaches between us again, and I glance down to see what she is doing.

For a split second I look away from the road and when I look back, we are already drifting off course. We are heading straight into another car. In a panic, I pull the steering wheel to correct my direction, and that is when everything goes wrong.

I lose control.

I brake hard and feel the car skid beneath us.

Suddenly, we collide with the hillside and I'm thrown forward onto the steering wheel. There's a high-pitched scream and a blur flashes past me just before the windshield shatters, and I instinctively cover my face with my arms.

Time slows down, and my body is thrown back against the car seat. It is eerily silent for a heartbeat.

"Oh, shit!" Panic laces Chase's voice. Dazed, I turn to look at him and see blood streaming from a cut on his head.

Then I turn to check on Harper.

She isn't there.

"Where's Harper?" I say as I look at the empty back row.

Chase grabs my shoulders and turns me to face him. "Are you okay? Are you hurt?"

I take a second to assess if I feel any pain. "I don't think so." I shake my head.

"We need to call nine-one-one." Chase reaches for his mobile and I turn to look around me and see the crumpled dash and the way the door is crushed beside me. I need to get out of this car. I need to find Harper.

I try to open the door, but it refuses to budge. We are stuck, and Harper is nowhere to be seen. My heart races, drowning out all other sounds. The car is a wreck. My parents will freak when they see it. They had trusted me to drive responsibly and now I have let them down.

"Harper!" I shouted her name into the air, but there is no reply. Where is she? My thoughts are jumbled and chaotic; why isn't she answering me? Suddenly, my eyes fall upon the hole in the windshield, and I remember something flying past me. I peer through the shattered glass, trying to make sense of the flickering car lights on the hillside.

That's when I see the blood.

CHAPTER TWO

18 Years Later

ayleigh

"THIS IS IT, kid. This is your last chance. Do the show or you're out." Brendon's voice thunders through the speaker of the phone.

The call ends abruptly, and I am left staring at the cell, fighting the urge to toss it against the wall and walk away from all of this. I look around at my apartment and all the awards and trophies I've earned over the years and wonder if it's really worth it.

Sure, I'm not a big deal in Nashville anymore, like I was a decade ago. At the peak of my career, I was performing in sold-out arenas around the world. How dare my manager threaten me like this?

"It can't be that bad." I turn to my assistant, Kelly, who wears a grim expression.

"Actually, it is."

I can't pinpoint when Kelly, who is in her twenties, joined my team. But I know she's endured a lot of hardship while working for me. Most assistants would have quit under the pressure, and many have over the years.

My life has been a wild ride, full of highs and lows. There have been men, alcohol, and drugs that constantly tempt me. Right now, I could really use a drink, or at least a cigarette, to calm my nerves.

"Damn it," I curse under my breath, running my hands over my forehead and across my scalp. My hair used to be full and curly, but now it is brittle and thin despite using products that promise to repair damaged strands. It serves as a constant reminder of the mistakes I have made by neglecting my own well-being.

"So, if I don't do this stupid show, my manager and the record company will drop me! Are you serious? It's absurd. I was the one who built up that damn label. Without me, they wouldn't even exist."

"It's only one show and probably a photo op." Kelly grips the back of the lounge chair, perhaps for protection should I start throwing things at her.

It wouldn't be the first time.

"But of all places! Why does it have to be there?" My stomach tenses at the mere thought of that town.

Sweetgum Valley.

"I haven't been back in eighteen years. Besides, I doubt they would even want me there."

"Are you kidding? That town has milked being the birthplace of the famous country music singer, Bayleigh Gilmore. It's doubled in size since you left."

"That's probably for the view." I remember the picturesque landscape of rolling hills and wooded parks. The town is known for its beautiful maple trees, poplars, and, of course, the vibrant sweetgum trees that give it its name. In fall, those trees put on a breathtaking show before shedding their leaves, creating a carpet of red and burgundy on the streets.

Pretty as it may be, it's not worth the pain it would cause me to return.

"I have too many bad memories of that place." The memories of my parents shouting at me—blaming me for the accident and telling me they would never forgive me.

Not that I could ever forgive myself. That one small moment, which altered not only my life but also the lives of all my family, is something I can never forgive myself for.

For a fleeting moment, I allow my thoughts to wander back to the days in Sweetgum Valley before the accident, when everything had been so perfect.

When I had . . . him.

The warmth of the sun enveloped us as we lay on the grass together in a meadow on his ranch. He traced a yellow flower over my face, causing me to laugh and revel in the soft sensation of its petals against my skin. His presence, along with the raw smell of earth and his own unique scent, drew me towards him like a magnet. I couldn't resist touching him; his shoulders were broad and muscular from playing football, his hair long and kissed by the sun, and his eyes deep brown pools. Looking at his beautiful face made me want to trust him completely, rely on him for everything, and surrender myself to him. He always made me feel safe when he was near.

The sudden, piercing scream shatters the memory and jolts me back to reality. That was the last sound I heard before everything changed. The cry of a pure, untainted soul. The cry of terror without restraint.

I sink into the soft cushions of the couch, allowing myself to be enveloped by its comfort. My eyes burn with tears and I press my palms against them, trying to block out the pain. How much longer will this torture continue? Will I be haunted for the rest of my life? Maybe it would be better to just end it.

I have attempted it multiple times. With alcohol, pills, and even a knife. But no matter how determined I've been, my attempts have always been unsuccessful.

"I'll get you a glass of water," Kelly says, and leaves the room.

The stinging sensation fades as I remove my hands.

Black streaks of mascara decorate my pale palms. I glance out the window at the Nashville skyline; the sunlight reflecting off the buildings.

I stand from the couch and make my way closer to the view, gazing out at the city sprawled beneath me. I have been living in Nashville for longer than I'd ever lived in Sweetgum Valley, but does it truly feel like home? When I left that small country town, I left behind my childhood, my family, and any sense of innocence. Singing was my escape and the only thing I was truly good at.

I'd thought I had been a great sister, too. But just look how that turned out.

Brendon had first pitched the idea of doing the Sweetgum Valley charity concert weeks ago, and I had been adamantly against it. Especially since I was fresh out of rehab for the, how many times is it now? Third or fourth? This time it is going to stick, though. There is too much riding on this.

What will they think of me? Bayleigh Gilmore, the has-been country singer. I used to bask in the spotlight; I was a household name. But now I am just a faded star from a small town with little to show for my success except for some shiny accolades and the physical reminders of my past battles.

I roll up the sleeves of my sweater and examine the faint scars that serve as a constant reminder of one of my many past mistakes. That moment was the turning point in my career, where I truly lost control. The moment I became reliant on anything other than myself, my fame began to dwindle. My unpredictable actions caused a rift between me and my band, my crew, and ultimately, my fans. After spending three months in rehab to get clean, I returned home to find my bank accounts drained and my record deal on the verge of being terminated.

"It's this or you're out, kid," Brendon's voice echoes. Kid has been his nickname for me since he had discovered me at an open mic night, not long after I arrived in the city. I have always trusted Brendon. Well, as much as I can trust anyone, at least. I should have listened to him the first time he told me to put down the needle and the booze.

But I didn't.

Maybe I should listen to him now. My entire career, my future, hinges on it. What will I do if I can no longer perform? With barely any money left, I'll have to search for a job. The thought of going back to waitressing is unbearable. I can't give up performing. Despite everything, my voice remains powerful and unwavering. Taking a break was beneficial, and I am ready for a new beginning.

But in Sweetgum Valley? I would happily go anywhere else.

"They're the only place that will take you," Brendon had said. "It will only be one night."

In and out in less than twenty-four hours wouldn't be so bad, would it? If I do a kick-ass performance, then others will want me and I can make my comeback bigger and better than I was when I first started.

"Here's your water," Kelly says, and I accept the glass from her.

"Call Brendon back and tell him to set up a meeting. I'm ready to hear more about this show in Sweetgum Valley."

Kelly raises her eyebrows in surprise. I am well aware of my reputation for being stubborn, and I take pride in it. I am known for being decisive and hate being told what to do.

But I also enjoy having a roof over my head and food to eat. Not that I eat that much these days, anyway. I am trying to get my appetite back and have started training with my PT again this week. No one wants to watch a shriveled up, gangly singer.

They want the star from ten years ago. Strong and fit with wild curls, cowgirl boots, and sparkling bodysuits.

I used to sing love songs that were hopeful and upbeat. Most of the time I had faked it on stage, never really believing that 'nothing could tear us apart' or 'all you need is love.' The lyrics are bullshit, made up by songwriters who get paid to write music for the naïve yet hopeful fans. They should have been writing songs for me about loss and heartbreak. Those are the types of songs I could get behind. No one wants to hear me sing those, though. These days, no one is writing songs for me at all.

Two hours and four cups of coffee later, I am sitting at my kitchen table, on a video call with the label rep—Dan and Brendon.

"The city council is raising funds for the farmers who are struggling with the drought. Apparently, it's been pretty dry for a few years now," Dan says. "It's a good cause and will make it look like you care."

"And Matthew Butler will be performing too. Plus a few smaller acts they are still confirming." Brendon leans into the camera so his face takes up more of the screen. Brendon has been like a father to me, spending more time with me than with his own family in the peak of my success. Little wonder his wife left him. In the recent years, though, he has spent less time focusing on me and more time with the new rising star, Matthew Butler.

I can hardly blame him, though. My career moves effect people than just me. My band, back-up singers, crew—all of them depend on me. I've failed them in the past and I want to make up for it now.

"Do they have any budget for my performance?" I ask, trying not to sound too desperate.

"They can offer you a small fee, but it's not much," Brendon replies.

I sigh and rub my temples. My financial situation isn't great, but I also don't want to sell myself short.

"It's not just about money," Dan chimes in. "Think about the exposure you'll get from performing."

I let the idea settle over me. It is a show for charity,

but a show that could do more for my career than anything else has in a long time. "Okay, as long as all I have to do is one concert." I hold up my finger to reinforce the number. "In and out. No staying in town for anything else."

Brendon shakes his head. "And one quick photo shoot of you around town with the mayor."

I open my mouth to interrupt, but Brendon continues speaking. "It will be good publicity. And we need all the good publicity we can get."

I sigh and slump back in the chair. "Fine. One photo shoot, sound check and the show. That's it."

A grin spreads over Brendon's face. "Thatta' girl. Show the fans that you're back and better than before."

"Then we can talk about a new album," Dan's thick Southern accent drawls out.

A surge of hope fills me. I yearn to be back in the spotlight, performing for a crowd of supporters and fans. Being on stage is my ultimate source of joy, where I can immerse myself in the music, the choreography, and the dazzling lights.

During a recent conversation with my sobriety coach, we talked about the potential for a new album to mark the start of a new chapter in my life as the improved version of Bayleigh Gilmore—now sober and determined to be better than ever.

"Alright, I'm in." I focus on the job ahead. I can do this.

It will be a quick in and out—no need to interact

with my parents or anyone from my past. I just need to focus on the show and then leave with only the memory of that performance. This will finally allow me to leave my past where it belongs—behind me.

"Good. We'll get the contract and send it to you soon," Brendon says. "Kelly will get the times for rehearsals. Get ready, Bayleigh. You leave in two weeks."

Two weeks. No time to waste. This is my big chance to make a comeback. And I plan to wow not just the crowd, but everyone.

ayleigh

I SMOOTH out my denim skirt as my uncovered legs stick to the leather seat of the private airplane. It is surreal to think that before I left Sweetgum Valley, I had never even been on a plane before, and now I am flying on one to perform a show. How much my life has changed since then.

We are twenty minutes into the fifty-minute flight to Sweetgum Valley, and I am still surprised to see the label has chartered a flight just for me. Kelly is there, of course, typing away on her laptop. But all the other plush, comfortable seats are empty.

"When is Matthew flying in? Why isn't he on this plane?"

Kelly looks up. "I'm not sure. Do you want me to find out?"

I shake my head. "No, I'm just curious." The handsome young man probably wants to make his own entrance alone. Not with a woman almost old enough to be his mother. *Almost.*

I reach into my bag and retrieve a compact mirror, then examine my reflection. At thirty-four, even with all of my makeup on, I can still see the wrinkles around my eyes. I silently curse myself for not getting Botox. Hopefully, the video cameras won't zoom in too closely and reveal my imperfections and flaws.

A crackle on the speaker signals the pilot is making an announcement. "We'll be landing in approximately ten minutes. If you look out the window on the right, you can see the town. We will be landing at a private airfield just north."

A lump forms in my throat. I have been trying not to think about this moment. I steel myself against whatever emotion I could have when I finally see my birthplace again. Being conveniently on the right side of the plane, I turn to stare out the window at the town sprawled below.

It is bigger than I had expected. Nowhere near the size of Nashville, of course, but certainly bigger than I remember. I try to find a familiar landmark, but it all looks different from up here.

My eyes are drawn to a sprawling housing development and nearby sports field. They must be new. The buildings have a modern design, in stark contrast to the old house I grew up in with my family.

Don't think about them.

I continue assessing the view. Is that my old school?

"Look at those fields!" Kelly says from opposite me. I look beyond the built-up area to the outlying farms. The fields are brown and mostly empty instead of crops painting the fields green the way I remember.

Out there somewhere, though, is the ranch I'd spent a lot of my youth at. That was where I'd learned to ride horses and where I'd helped with branding. I wonder if the Tuttons are one of the families doing it tough in this drought. Hard to imagine they haven't been touched by this tragic turn of nature.

"No wonder this concert is so important to them." Kelly returns her attention to the laptop in front of her and the town drifts under us as the pilot starts the descent.

"Brendon has a car waiting and we're to go to the Claremont Hotel first." All business, Kelly starts to pack her belongings and put them in her bag.

I check my reflection in the compact once more and, satisfied, return it to my bag. "Why are we going to a hotel if we're only here for a few hours? I thought we were flying straight back to Nashville?"

Kelly shrugs. "Brendon said that's where the mayor is going to meet you."

The plane lands, and I stand and smooth the crinkles out of my skirt. Knee-high tan cowgirl boots keep my legs warm on the cool fall day. I wear a black long-sleeve top and a pale scarf around my neck. "How do I look?" I turn to Kelly.

"May I?" Kelly raised her hand toward my hair and when I nod, Kelly gently pulls a section of long blond curls over my shoulder. "The hairdresser did such a good job."

I don't know exactly what the hairdresser spent such a long time doing, but I do know my hair is now looking more like it used to, with the addition of extensions and some serious conditioning treatments.

The flight attendant ushers us toward the stairs, and I step out to see a small crowd of people with their cameras and phones raised to capture the first images of me out in public in almost four months.

I take a deep breath, plaster on that sparkling smile, and wave. People cheer and call out to me as I step down onto the tarmac. A young girl who couldn't be more than eight holds out a poster in one hand and a pen in the other.

I walk over to the barrier separating us. "Hi, would you like me to sign that?"

The girl nods, a huge, starstruck smile on her face.

I take the poster and look at the picture. It was taken at least nine years ago. I vaguely remember the photoshoot. I'm wearing my signature cowgirl boots—this time with tassels—super-short denim shorts and a white crop top. The pose is sexy and provocative. I wonder why this girl's mother let her bring *that* photo.

"What's your name, sweetheart?"

"Lily," the girl replies.

I write her name and then sign mine, just as I have millions of times, adding a heart in place of the dot in the *i* in Bayleigh.

"Can we get a photo?" a man with a professional camera calls out.

"Would you like a photo?" I ask Lily, who nods excitedly.

Security opens a gap in the barrier and Lily joins me. The girl snuggles in close as the photographer snaps away. Then Lily is escorted back to her mother as I move on to sign more autographs and pose for more pictures.

Finally, I wave goodbye to the fans and climb into the waiting black car. Kelly sits next to me and the driver takes us towards the town.

"That was really good. Nice move with the little girl." Kelly smiles.

"She was so cute. But that picture of me that she had." I cringe. "Glad they don't make me pose like that anymore."

The landscape changes as we leave the desolate farmlands and enter the bustling town. The street is filled with a mix of old buildings that have been updated with modern touches and new structures adorned with flashy signs. We pass by a charming diner with outdoor seating, a boutique clothing store with an unfamiliar name, and even an art gallery showcasing a stunning wooden chaise lounge in its front window. As our car halts at a red light outside it, I can't help but admire the intricate woodwork on the piece of furniture. It is truly a work of art, and I wonder if it would be as comfortable to recline on as it appears.

"Is it how you remember?" Kelly asks, following my gaze.

"Not really." I pull my attention away from the store and take in the rest of the busy street. "There used to be a movie theatre there." I sigh. The once entertainment hub is now a common department store. The memories of family outings for dinner and a movie are quickly pushed aside.

The car moves again and soon after pulls up in front of the Claremont Hotel and I climb out to be welcomed by a porter and another man. The building is as grand as any hotel in New York, and I can't help but be impressed by the inviting couches and soft lighting.

"Welcome to Sweetgum Valley, Ms. Gilmore. I'm Ian Dobson, the hotel manager." A man in a crisp suit with the hotel's logo emblazoned on the jacket holds out his hand.

I shake it with a smile. "Thank you. This is a lovely hotel."

"It was recently re-opened after being renovated. You are our first VIP guest, so if there is anything we can do for you, please just ask."

"Oh, I'm not staying, but thank you for the offer."

I catch the confused look on his face before Kelly gestures for me to follow her. We head to the elevator and Kelly pushes the button for the top floor.

"Where are we going now?" I ask.

"To freshen up while we wait. Brendon said he'd call when the mayor was on his way." Although she seems confident, I have the distinct impression she is just as perplexed as me. In a few hours we will be wheels up, heading back to Nashville, so why are we wasting time here? I'm eager to get to soundcheck and get ready for the show.

I follow along as Kelly swipes the key over the penthouse door card reader and opens the double doors for me. The suite has the same luxurious-but-friendly feel as the lobby. There is a large sitting area with a table for four by the window. I wander over to see the view. Below me sits the town of Sweetgum Valley. It is bigger than before, at least twice the size now with commercial businesses and shops lining the streets. The hotel is the highest building at four floors and I can easily see the main street below. It is wide, with a strip of central parking down the middle splitting the main drag into a divided road. Cars bake under the fall sun as the locals go about their business. The people are walking along the streets at a relaxed speed, not in any sort of hurry like they are in Nash-ville. The pace here is slower than in a city, as though the residents want to take in all their surroundings and not miss a thing.

Behind me, I hear Kelly answer the phone and I turn. I haven't bothered getting a new cell for myself since losing mine before going to rehab. Kelly is always with me and takes care of the running of my life. I am glad not to be connected like everyone else with distractions constantly buzzing and interrupting me.

Kelly takes the phone from her ear and holds it out for me. "It's Brendon. He wants to speak to you."

I brush my hair away from my ear before lifting the phone. "Hi Brendon. I'm here. What are we waiting for? We've got a show to do."

"Hi Bayleigh." Brendon's voice sounds worried. I know that tone and brace myself for whatever bad news he is about to deliver.

"So, you do have a photo shoot to do, but, well, the concert isn't tonight."

"What do you mean? It's Saturday; it's supposed to be tonight. Did it get cancelled or something?"

"No, it's going ahead. It's planned for next Saturday."

I let out a gasp. "Who got the bloody date wrong? Do we need to fly back next week?"

"No, no one screwed up." He pauses. "You are booked to stay there until next Sunday. You have events and interviews to do all week. It'll be a great way for you to slowly get used to being back in the public eye."

"What the fuck, Brendon? I signed a contract for one photo shoot and a concert!"

"Actually, you signed a contract for a week."

Furiously, I spin on my heel to face Kelly, who looks just as shocked as me. "We agreed to—"

"You can check it if you want. Kelly has the email with the signed contract," Brendon continues, using his all-business tone. "You still need to take it slowly and ease back into it. Walk around town and meet some fans. Look like you give a shit about the place. Some good publicity is what you need right now to win back your fans."

"You fucking lied to me. You know I don't read all the contract. You knew that and let me sign it, anyway." I want to scream at him, to my whole damn team who have manipulated me into this. They knew I wanted to spend as little time as possible in this town and they have purposely connived me into being here a whole week. "I'm not going to stay. I don't care if I have to fly bloody economy class, I'm not spending a week here!

"If you don't stay there, you will be in breach of contract." Brendon's tone is stern. "Remember what I said—if you don't do this concert, you are finished. No one will ever sign you again." He sighs. "I'm sorry about the misunderstanding, but you're there now. Just do the job, play nice, have a great concert, and get on with it. Remember the new album you want? This will get it for you."

"I am so sick of people telling me what to do. For fuck's sake, I'm a grown woman."

"The last time we let you do what you wanted, you ended up in rehab with a reputation for being unstable. We're trying to help you. *I'm* trying to help you."

I want to scream. I hate the lot of them.

Being stuck in Sweetgum Valley is my worst nightmare. I can't bear the thought of running into anyone from my past, especially with the constant threat of the press discovering the truth. The label has worked hard to keep my departure from the town a secret, but what if that all comes crashing down? Then again, could my reputation really get any worse? I am already known as a drug addict with two failed marriages under my belt. I feel like I have hit rock bottom. Is there even room to fall any farther?

"You really think being seen here will be good publicity?"

"We do. Walk around town; do some friendly interviews. Plus, you can practice and prepare for the concert. Make sure your head is in the game."

A heavy sigh escapes my lips as I realize there is no way out of this situation. I have to follow Brendon's advice and play nice, even though the thought scares me. My future hinges on my ability to do so. But deep down, I am afraid of what might happen if I let myself fully remember and open up that part of my heart again. It is a risk I'm not sure I am willing to take.

I hand the phone back to Kelly and she looks at me in apology. "I swear I didn't know, Bayleigh."

I had trusted Brendon and not bothered to read the contract myself. I should have and I regret that decision now.

Kelly gives me an apologetic look. "I'm going out to run some errands. We have a dinner to go to tonight, and I need to pick up some things now that we're staying longer. Why don't you stay here and have a bath? Maybe meditate?"

She is right—that plan sounds perfect. She understands my needs more than I do myself. And I have to admit, her stunning hourglass figure and long legs are easy on the eye. She's been by my side through the toughest times, and even though she is technically paid to take care of me, we've also become good friends.

While she is out, I sit on the floor and meditate to my favorite binaural beats playlist. I picked up a lot of techniques in rehab, and this has been one of the best ways to help me when I am feeling stressed. Afterwards, I take a long soak in the spa bath and lather myself in the lotion the hotel has provided. From looking at the label, I know it was made locally, which makes me smile. This town is more than just crops and beef now.

"Feel better?" Kelly asks when she returns to my room, her hands loaded with bags.

"Much." I smile at her, definetly more Zen after the self-care regime.

"Good. I got you something." She holds up her arms. "Actually, I got you lots of things, but this is the one I mean." She waves a smaller bag at me and I take it from her. Looking inside, I see a cell phone.

"I think you've earned it," Kelly says with a grin.

While I had missed my phone a little, being without one has been kind of freeing. There is no temptation to endlessly scroll or read what the media is saying.

She must see the trepidation going through mind. "Don't worry—I had them set it up at the shop. There are no apps except your personal email, and you can't download anything without my permission."

"So you're giving me a kids phone?" I grin. I am grateful to not have to deal with the temptation. I could probably still scroll the internet, and that is bad enough.

Kelly wags her finger at me. "It's for emergencies only."

I mock salute her. "Yes, ma'am."

"Now that's settled, let me show you what I got!" Kelly says with a cheeky rise of her eyebrows.

* * *

"I HATE THESE DINNERS." I sigh as I wash my hands in the restroom.

Kelly hands me some paper towels. "I know you do,

but, like Brendon said, its great publicity. Plus, that steak really was good."

I check my appearance in the mirror. Kelly has organized an entire wardrobe for me now that I am staying longer and haven't packed enough. She's even had my favorite brand of cowgirl boots shipped in by courier. Kelly is the best assistant and friend I have ever had—she seems to be able to work miracles at a moment's notice. Although she hadn't been able to get me out of this week-long visit.

I resolve to just make the most of it and work on my music. After following Kelly back through the crowded restaurant, I rejoin the group of event organizers at their table. I make sure to smile and nod when appropriate and avoid sharing strong opinions on the topics being discussed.

"Are you excited to spend some time with your family while you're home?" Julia, the young woman sitting to my left, asks as we sip coffee.

The word *home* is enough to stop me in my tracks. Sweetgum Valley hasn't been my home in eighteen years and I sure as hell am not excited about even the possibility of running into my family or any other relation from my past. So I just give Julia a tight smile. "Mm-hmm."

Finally, Kelly signals dinner is over by standing and helping me into my jacket.

I obligingly shake hands and show my appreciation

to everyone for inviting me to the concert and having me for dinner.

As we walk through the restaurant to the exit, I see several people pull out their phones and film me. I plaster on my best smile and wave at a couple of girls who call out, "We love you."

The noise from the restaurant is soon replaced by the sound of live music as we get out the door. I look around the street to see where it is coming from.

"There's live music at Monty's. A local band plays there every Saturday night. The town loves it," Julia explains, and points to a neon sign a few shops away.

I pause to listen as the band plays a familiar ballad. "That's country music."

"Not much demand for anything other than country in Sweetgum Valley," she says. "Tickets to your show sold out within a few hours of going on sale. Everyone wants to see you and Matthew Butler live, and support a worthy cause, of course."

Kelly turns to me and in a low voice, says, "We should go in and listen for a while. Brendon would love that. Especially with all the press following."

I am super-aware of the cameras filming my every move, and Kelly's suggestion would certainly build my image in a positive way.

"Okay," I agree, turning and saying good night to my dinner hosts, and then following Kelly.

The sound of the music grows louder as we get closer to the door, and I can distinguish every chord and note from the guitar. A man is singing an old Garth Brooks tune, and the crowd is clapping and joining in on the lyrics. I can't help but smile at how much the audience seems to be loving it.

As Kelly pushes open the door, we are met with a wall of people crammed into the packed room. Every table is occupied and I only catch a glimpse of the stage amidst the crowd. The scent of beer lingers in the air, almost suffocatingly strong.

As soon as a few members of the crowd spot me, a murmur begins to spread and fingers start pointing in my direction. People quickly move aside to make room for me to pass, and some even offer their seats at a nearby table. I smile gratefully and thank them before inviting them to join us. A waitress appears and asks if I would like a drink, so I request a sweet tea and then turned towards the stage just in time to catch the end of the band's song.

The lead singer is a handsome man, younger than me, with neatly coiled black hair and a glimmer in his eye that could make any girl weak at the knees.

At the end of the song, he speaks into the mic. "I see we have a special guest here tonight." A round of clapping and whistling sounds follow. I smile and look around at the excited faces. I have missed this—the appreciation, the love. I live for my fans and the support they show me. Suddenly I don't feel so sick about having to spend the week there. If I get this kind of welcome everywhere I go, it will be worth it.

"On behalf of everyone in Sweetgum Valley, I would like to welcome you, Bayleigh Gilmore, to town!"

My focus shifts back to the stage, and I am just about to call out my appreciation when my gaze lands on the guitarist next to the singer. He'd had his back to me a moment ago, but now I can make out his features distinctly.

That face.

That hair.

That body.

He may have aged, but time has been kind to him. So very, very kind.

Our eyes meet, and it seems as though no one else exists as I drink him in.

It has been eighteen years and yet my body is still physically reacting to him. Wanting his touch.

He is still here—living in Sweetgum Valley, despite our grand plans to make it in the music industry. Here he is, with that guitar slung over his shoulder and his faded blue jeans, looking sexy as all hell.

Kelly nudges me out of my trance and nods to the stage.

"What?" I ask, having missed whatever the lead singer said.

"He wants you to sing. He's invited you up."

"No, I can't do that." I shake my head, still spinning from seeing *him*.

"You can't say no now. You kinda have to!" Kelly says with that look on her face that said she wouldn't take no for an answer, and she stands up so I can pass. In the time it takes for me to walk to the stage, I try my hardest to regain my composure.

I can do this. I hope.

"Hi, I'm Frankie," the singer says to me away from the mic. "We know all your songs. What would you like to sing?"

"You do?" I can't help liking Frankie and his confidence. Then I turn to see Chase and find him standing in the shadow, watching me.

I name the song and take the mic. "Thank y'all for inviting me to town. I didn't intend to sing tonight—I just wanted to watch this band." I wave my hand at Frankie and the other band members. "They sounded real good from outside, so I wanted to come in and join y'all."

The sound of the crowd's applause and cheers washes over me, and I feel a sense of relief. The stage has always felt like my sanctuary. Making people laugh and smile is what I was born to do—my true calling in life.

From just behind me, I hear the acoustic guitar intro for my most famous song start, and I know it is Chase. I listen to the way he strums his guitar in that hypnotic way of his.

I begin to sing the heart-wrenching love ballad that won me my first Grammy. As I close my eyes and pour all of my emotion into the lyrics, the room falls silent except for the sound of my voice and his guitar. It feels just like old times, when it was just the two of us making music together.

The sound of drums fills the room, followed by the bass. Frankie begins to harmonize and I am lost in the music. The way each instrument complements and elevates the others is perfection. The lyrics are powerful and the notes flow seamlessly together. I pour my heart into my performance, and when I finish my final note, I open my eyes to see the audience on their feet, clapping and cheering.

I beam at them, feeling a sense of excitement and joy that I haven't experienced in years. I return the mic to Frankie and thank him before making my way back to the table. Along the way, people stop me to snap photos and ask for autographs as the band resumes playing. Finally, I reach my seat where Kelly is grinning at me and holding out her phone. "You did amazing!" she exclaims.

The video of my performance plays across the screen, though I can't hear it over the noise around us. I see myself singing, being swept away in the music. And I see Chase. He doesn't take his eyes off me the whole song.

Fuck. How am I going to make it through the week knowing he is still in town?

I turn back to the stage and watch him play, but try to avoid direct eye contact. What is he doing these days? Is he in a relationship? Does he still think about me?

Years of unanswered questions swarm in my mind.

The thought of talking to him fills me with fear, but I cannot deny the urge. The girl he once knew is not the same as the one sitting here. I will never be that naïve and trusting child again.

I finish my drink and tell Kelly I am ready to go. I can feel his gaze on me as we make our way out of the bar, the band's music fading into the background as his intense stare follows me all the way.

CHAPTER FOUR

hase

I LET my guitar hang loosely by my side as I take a sip of ice-cold water. The crowd at Monty's is electric tonight, and it is fueling our performance. We thrive on their energy and the more they cheer, the better we play. Frankie, our expert performer, is especially engaging with the audience, and he's building them up more than usual. It is clear in the way they cheer at the end of our last song; their enthusiasm almost drowns out the sound of the drums.

After setting the bottle down, I wipe my mouth with the back of my hand and turn to face the stage for the next number. That is when I notice the audience suddenly becoming animated. I hear Frankie's voice amplified through the microphone: "Bayleigh Gilmore!" He points towards a table in the center of the room, and my heart skips a beat when I lay eyes on her.

In an instant, I am filled with recognition as I see her long blonde curls and the face that used to consume my thoughts every day during my youth. Her smile is familiar, yet it holds a new depth that wasn't there before. It has been what, eighteen years since I've gazed into those eyes, and though she is still undeniably beautiful, there is a sense of lingering sadness in her appearance now. She is no longer the innocent child I once knew.

I've kept up with her career, as has the whole town —her successes and failures, highs and lows. And now, she is headed towards the stage. I can't help but notice how her jeans cling to her thighs, reminding me of how smooth they've felt under my touch.

Frankie hands her the microphone before coming over to stand next to me. "Can you believe it? Bayleigh Gilmore is going to join us in singing 'Maybe, Darling!'" He beams at me. "No pressure, bro. This will go viral by tomorrow." The weight of his words settles on my shoulders as I take a deep breath.

I quickly sift through my thoughts to find the music for her first hit single. I've listened to every one of her songs, willingly or not. Every chord change and every beat is etched into my memory, as if she's performed each lyric just for me.

I begin strumming the guitar, and my fingers move

effortlessly over the strings, driven by muscle memory. As she starts singing, the room falls silent, except for my guitar and her mesmerizing voice.

My gaze remains fixed on her and I sense the exact moment when she relaxes and becomes lost in the music, and I am drawn in with her. Together, we remain entranced for the duration of the song. Memories, dreams, and regrets drift over me like passing clouds. But just as quickly as it starts, the song ends, and she turns to face me. Our eyes meet and I cannot bring myself to break the connection.

She walks off the stage and returns to her seat. My heart aches as I watch her, wishing I could run after her and talk to her. There are so many questions I want to ask, so many things I want to say. But as she sits at her table, I realize that the hole she's left in my heart has never truly been filled. Seeing her again, being this close, only makes it more apparent.

I'm not over Bayleigh Gilmore. And I don't think I ever will be.

For the next two songs, I can't take my eyes off of her. Every note I play is tinged with grief, knowing that she may never be mine again. But our eyes keep meeting, as if we are still connected somehow.

And then, just like before, she leaves without waiting for me to finish my set. She walks out the door, just like she did all those years ago. And this time, I wonder if it is really goodbye. Will she ever walk back into my life again?

I am well aware that she will be performing at the upcoming charity concert. The entire town of Sweetgum Valley has been buzzing about it for weeks. I've mentally prepared myself to avoid her at all costs. Attending the concert is not on my agenda, and in fact, after tonight, I plan to go back to the ranch and throw myself into work there. I don't want to have to hear about her or constantly be reminded that we are only miles apart from each other. My mind is made up—as soon as our set finishes, I'll gather my belongings and make a swift exit from Sweetgum Valley, and I won't return until she's left it far behind.

Then I can return to the monotonous existence I've created for myself. The physical ache for her is manageable—I've survived without it for a long time now. But the emotional ties with Bayleigh are too strong. We've had too many shared memories and intimate moments. She's been by my side for half of my life, and we've formed countless core memories together. Losing her was the most excruciating pain I've ever experienced. I never want to go through something like that again. That is why I won't put myself in a vulnerable position with her or anyone else. This time, maybe I can find the closure I've been yearning for all these years.

After our set, I am putting my guitar into the case when Frankie slaps me on the back. The man has been buzzing all night. As hard as the evening has been for me, I know this could have a major effect on my bandmates, who, unlike me, are very ambitious and hope to make music their career.

"Check out this video, bro!" Frankie shoves his phone screen in my face, and I can't help but watch Bayleigh singing into the microphone again.

"It's great, man. I really hope something comes of it for you," I say with as much enthusiasm as I can muster.

"How fucking lucky were we? I mean, who would have expected her to walk into Monty's tonight while we were playing?" Frankie practically dances with excitement.

I return Frankie's smile, grateful for his friendship. He moved to Sweetgum Valley as a teenager, seven years younger than me. Unlike most people in town, he doesn't know about my past with Bayleigh. Bayleigh and I used to be childhood friends and more, but now that feels like a distant memory that no one dares to mention. It ended long ago, and yet, I can still feel the sensation of her hair slipping through my fingers, reminding me it was once real and not just a figment of my imagination.

"Aren't you thrilled about this opportunity? It could be huge for all of us!" Frankie says.

I sling my guitar case over my shoulder. "I'm genuinely happy for you and the rest of the band. But you know I'm not chasing after those kinds of dreams like you are."

"We couldn't have made it this far without you,

man. That intro, when it was just you and her playing together . . . I can't even put into words how amazing it sounded."

"Really?" I'd thought the moment had just been in my own head.

"Really. It was like y'all had hypnotized us. Crazy!" Frankie laughs and taps the screen of his phone. "I've sent you the video. Will you stay for a drink?"

My phone buzzes in my back pocket. "Nah, I got to get home. Need an early night cause I'm working in the gallery tomorrow. I'll talk to you in a few days."

"Bro, you can't leave now! You gotta help us. Media and influencers will be swarming this place. We gotta make the most of it. Play more gigs."

I shake my head. "I can't. Ask Davy instead; he can play acoustic just as well."

But Frankie won't give up, his big brown eyes pleading with me. "Please, we really need you. You're the best."

"Hey, guys." Carlos, the owner of Monty's, interrupts us. "I just had a call from Bayleigh Gilmore's manager. Her label is interested in talking to you."

Frankie's jaw drops so low, I am worried I'll have to scoop it up off the floor.

"Already?" Frankie asks.

"Yep, got the call just after you played together. Her assistant called her manager during the set, and he heard y'all over the phone."

"Holy shit!" Frankie pulls me into an awkward side-hug. "Bro, I will do anything you want if you stay."

I let out a sigh. I could never refuse my friend. Especially since he has always had my back and tolerates my flaws without judgement.

"Okay, let me know what you need."

"Yes!" Frankie hugs me again, then hugs Carlos, and anyone else he can get his arms around.

Carlos turns his gaze towards me. He is a local, raised in this town, just like many others. He is well aware of Bayleigh's history. "That was an incredible song," he says, breaking the silence. "You're a good man for helping him."

I give him a small smile. "Thank you."

As Carlos leaves, I can't help but ponder: if I truly am a good man, why did Bayleigh choose to leave me behind?

CHAPTER FIVE

ayleigh

"I NEED COFFEE," I grizzle as I zombie-walk out of the bedroom the following morning.

In a matter of seconds, Kelly is by my side with a cup of black coffee in her hand. I take a sip, but the bitter taste makes me grimace. "There has to be better coffee in this town," I say as I pass the cup back to Kelly and turn to look out the window. The streets are bustling below, filled with people going about their day.

"Did you sleep well?" Kelly asks, standing beside me.

"Not really," I admit. In truth, thoughts of Chase kept me tossing and turning all night.

"It's only a few days, and it'll be over before you know it." My assistant is ever the optimist. "Once you're ready, we'll go out for breakfast and be seen around town, looking at the shops."

"That shouldn't take very long." I run my gaze up the street. Although there are new shops and businesses, Sweetgum Valley is still a small town—not exactly a shopping mecca. I doubt they even have a mall. When Target opened, it was a big deal to the townsfolk. "Alright, but first, coffee."

Kelly helps me dress into light blue jeans and a chic boho shirt. I am well known for my boho/country/chic look and my signature cowgirl boots. I have built my image on being a stylish country music star who loves tassels and scarves. The style has always suited my blonde curls, which I usually wear down.

With my makeup in place and a tan purse slung across my body, I follow Kelly out of the suite.

"This is Max." She gestures to the large, bald man, dressed all in black, standing in front of the door. "He's your new bodyguard."

"Hey, how you doing?" I smile at him and walk toward the lift, Kelly and Max close behind me.

As a celebrity, privacy is often hard to come by. However, after years of living in the public eye, I have grown accustomed to the constant presence of security. There are always fans who push boundaries and disregard personal space. I've had my share of creepy stalkers.

When we walk out of the lift into the lobby, a man in a grey suit approaches us with a friendly wave. "Ms. Gilmore!"

I recognize him as the hotel manager who greeted us upon arrival, so I pause and let him catch up to us.

"Ms. Gilmore, I want to ensure that your accommodations are satisfactory. Is there anything I can do to assist you?" Mr. Dobson asks politely.

I turn to Kelly with a questioning look. "I believe everything is fine. Don't you agree?"

Kelly nods in agreement. "Thank you, Mr. Dobson. Your hotel is lovely."

"We're honored to have you as our guest," he says with a friendly smile and pride in his voice.

"Thank you," Kelly replies, motioning for us to continue walking. I force a smile as we exit the lobby and step onto the street. A cool breeze tousles my hair and I quickly brush it away from my face. The air smells fresh and clean, a welcome change from the constant scent of gasoline in the city.

With her phone in hand, Kelly leads us down the street to a diner with outdoor seating and umbrellas for shade. "Inside or outside?" she asks me.

"It's a bit chilly out here. Let's go inside." I turn the handle and push open the door, causing the bell above it to jingle. As we step into the cozy bistro, I am surrounded by natural light and shelves filled with lush green plants that add to the warm atmosphere. Most of the tables are occupied by couples and families enjoying their Sunday breakfast together. The tempting scents of freshly brewed coffee and warm biscuits fill the air, making my stomach growl loudly.

Max pulls out a chair for me at a table near the wall, then stands behind me where he can watch. A nervous waitress comes over to take our coffee orders, glancing at me every few seconds. I can feel the stares and whispers from the other patrons around us as they take photos and giggle amongst themselves.

"Did this place exist when you were young?" Kelly inquires.

I try to remember. "No, the diner is a recent addition. It used to be the old post office."

So much has changed here. It doesn't feel like the Sweetgum Valley I once knew. But surprisingly, not everything here triggers memories of my past life like I'd thought it would.

Our drinks arrive just in time, preventing me from delving too deeply into my memories. If I let them surface, they will consume me and I won't be able to push them back down again. The past is best left where it belongs, so I can focus on shaping my future.

I take a long sip of my coffee and let out a contented sigh as its warmth travels down my throat. This is some seriously good coffee.

"We have some emails to go through." Kelly pulls out her iPad and we work as we nibble on buttery pastries. I'm on my second cup of coffee when I hear the door jingle and look up.

Chase strides confidently up to the counter and speaks quietly to the waitress. She responds with a smile, and her hand briefly touches his arm in a gesture that I find irritatingly intimate. As she turns to the coffee machine, Chase's gaze follows her before turning toward me.

Our gazes meet and lock. My heart races as he continues to look at me, furrowing his strong brows. The stubble on his square jaw catches my attention, along with the way his Adam's apple moves under the collar of his khaki jacket.

"That's the guitar player from last night." Kelly says it more like a statement that a question, and I turn and see the lustful gaze on my assistant's face. "He's cute. Do you know him?"

"I used to," I say, placing my hand on my scarf and recognizing the familiar shape of my pendant under my fingers. Looking up at Chase through my lowered lashes, I hope he will avert his gaze, yet I also want to keep staring into those hypnotic blue eyes.

The waitress finishes preparing his takeaway coffee and hands it to him. He gives me one last glance before exiting the diner.

With him gone, the diner suddenly feels empty. Where does he live? What is he doing now? These questions have been plaguing me all night. Is he with someone? Is he happy?

After finishing my coffee, I turn to Kelly and ask, "What's next on our agenda?"

A smile spreads across Kelly's face. "Shopping time!"

* * *

A SIZABLE AMOUNT of money has been forwarded for me to spend in the town, so Kelly and I take advantage by spending the next hour browsing the trendy women's clothing store next to the diner. Max, as watchful as I'd expect, waits outside for us. I try on various new jeans and tops, adding them to our ever-growing pile of items we can't leave without. The store's unique blend of country and sparkling fashion has caught my eye and the attentive shop assistant helps me find sizes and make suggestions as I try on almost everything in sight.

"Wow, you should definitely wear that on Saturday," Kelly exclaims as I stare at myself in the full-length mirror. The white dress has just enough diamantes to be showy but not tacky. The outfit is loose and easy to move in.

"I think it needs something." I purse my lips and look around the shop. "That belt," I point to a hanger. "The brown one."

The assistant rushes to grab the accessory and hands it to me, its buckle a striking turquoise color. I fasten it around my waist and smooth out any wrinkles. Kelly gives a nod of approval. I gather my long hair off my back and let it cascade in soft curls over my shoulders..

"I can't wait to see the show," the assistant, who couldn't be more than twenty-one, says. "I got my ticket just as soon as they went on sale."

I smile at her. "Thank you. I appreciate your support."

"You're just so loved around here. We're so proud to be the hometown of Bayleigh Gilmore."

I return the smile, the weight of being an icon in this town on my shoulders. After changing back into my regular clothes Kelly pays for my purchases and we continue walking down the street. I can't help but look into the windows of the shops, noticing how different their interiors appear compared to how they looked when I lived in this town.

I pause abruptly when I recognize the ornately carved chaise at the entry to a gallery. "This is that art gallery I saw from the car. Let's go in there." I open the glass door and step inside, Kelly obediently following.

The scents of wood and polish fill the shop, and I take a deep breath to savor them. My eyes wander around the room, taking in all the unique crafts and artwork on display. The walls are adorned with paint-ings and drawings, but it's the wooden pieces that capture my attention. From tables and chairs to chess-boards and cutlery, each one is proudly showcased. As I run my fingers over the back of a love seat, I am struck by the smoothness of the wood beneath my touch.

"Look at the craftsmanship," I remark, admiring the intricate details of the design. A tree of life, its roots stretching out in every direction, has been artfully carved into the center of the seat. Suddenly, a thought crosses my mind: me sitting in this chair, humming a tune and jotting down lyrics in a notebook. But where did that come from? I haven't written any music since I left.

"Can I help with anything?" a man's voice asks from behind me and I gulp. No way.

"Oh, it's you! Is this your store?" Kelly asks as I slowly spin around to see Chase standing behind the till.

He gives a small shake of his head and then turns to Kelly to clarify. "I have partial ownership in the gallery, along with all the other artists. We take turns managing it and working here."

Kelly lets out a playful giggle. "Lucky us! Which pieces are yours?"

He clears his throat before answering. "I specialize in woodwork—furniture and smaller creations."

Our eyes meet and my breath catches in my throat. His skin is bronzed and stubble shadows his jawline. Wearing faded denim jeans and a plaid shirt, he is the embodiment of the sexy cowboy.

"So, you're both a musician and a craftsman?" Kelly is already making her way over to him. "Such impressive skills!"

"Thanks." Chase's gaze leaves mine to focus on

Kelly as she continues to gush at him. "I wish I had more time to work on my art, but I have a ranch just out of town that I run."

The question slips out of my mouth before I can hold it back. "What happened to your dad running the ranch? He used to be in charge there."

A shadow passes over Chase's face, sadness lingering in the depths of his dark eyes. "My father passed away a few years ago, so I had to step up and take over. Otherwise, we would have lost the ranch." His attention shifts towards Kelly. "It's been in our family for generations."

Kelly expresses her sympathy, placing a comforting hand on his arm.

I have to stop her.

She can't flirt with Chase like this, especially not in front of me. Every time she bats her eyelashes at him, it feels like nails on a chalkboard.

"Kelly, could you wait for me outside?" I ask her, hoping she'll take the hint.

With a frown, she turns to face me.

"I'll just be a minute," I say, gesturing towards Max waiting near the glass door.

"Oh, okay," Kelly mutters as she walks by.

I swallow hard, the weight of all our unresolved issues hanging over me. I had hoped to avoid running into Chase in this small town, but fate seems determined to bring us together. I sigh, resigning myself to the awkward conversation that needs to happen now. I take a few hesitant steps towards Chase, who still stands frozen in place.

"We keep seeing each other." I try to say it as a joke, but it falls like a dead weight between us.

"Yeah, small town," he says. His voice hasn't changed; it's still deep and throaty, reminding me of all the moments when he confided his secrets and dreams.

I take another step closer, grateful that the shop is empty so no one can eavesdrop on us. "I was wondering if you were still here. You never left?"

He shakes his head slightly. "I moved away for a little while, but then I came back. Not like you, though. You really made it big."

"Yeah, well, for a while at least." I shove my hands into the pockets of my jeans and glance around the shop. "Did you really make all this?"

He finally steps out from behind the table and cautiously approaches me. "Yep. Went into carpentry after high school, and we opened this place a couple of years ago."

"You were always so skilled with your hands." I instantly regret saying it, but my words bring a small smile to his face. "I'm glad you kept playing guitar. You always had a lot of talent."

He waves in my direction. "And now you're here to play for us. I'm surprised you're staying for so long."

"It was only supposed to be a quick appearance, but my manager wants me to do some press while I'm here and improve my public image."

Chase moves closer, narrowing the space between us. "I think your image is great as it is."

My eyes flicker to his lips, recalling the sensation of them against mine and on other parts of my body. "Chase, I . . ."

Before I can finish my thought, Kelly interrupts from the doorway with her phone held out. "Brendon's on the line for you."

"Just a moment." I turn back to Chase. "I should probably take that call."

"Wait, Bayleigh."

The way he says my name sends a flurry of emotions through me. He grasps my arm gently, but his touch makes me flustered. For a moment, we just stand there, looking into each other's eyes. He wants answers from me, but I am not ready to give them.

Then he lets go and steps back. "Have a good show," he says.

"Thanks," I reply, walking away before I do something impulsive. "It was nice to see you."

"Bye," he says as I hurry out of the shop, dodging furniture and displays in my rush for fresh air. Once I am out the door and back onto the quiet street, I stop and take a deep breath with my eyes closed before exhaling slowly.

"Are you alright?" Kelly asks, walking over to me.

"Yes, I'm fine," I respond, pushing down my feelings. This is not the time to dwell on the past. Chase belongs there, and that's where he should stay.

CHAPTER SIX

hase

FUCK ME.

I stare at the gallery door, still in shock after Bayleigh's departure. I had known it would be strange to have her back in town, but I never expected to keep running into her like this. And each time, she affects me deeply.

We are no longer kids. We have both grown into adults and are living our own separate lives She shouldn't still have such a strong hold over me.

Growing up I only had eyes for Bayleigh. No other girl could compare to her when it came to her beauty, intelligence, and passion for music. We were only ten when she announced we were starting a band, and she gave me the choice of playing guitar or drums. Guitar seemed like the easier and cheaper option, so I learned it. But practicing never felt like a chore because I loved the instrument and loved playing alongside her as she sang. Making music together felt like the most natural thing in the world, and even when her little sister Harper joined us, I didn't mind sharing the stage. With Bayleigh's soprano and Harper's alto voice blending perfectly together, they turned heads whenever they performed. It was clear their talent ran in the family.

Then they asked me to harmonize as well. It added another dimension to our music, taking us to new heights of seriousness. We began dreaming about our future musical careers, confident that success was within reach. With every performance and practice session, we inched closer towards our goals. But then it all fell apart. In the blink of an eye, everything changed. One moment was all it took. One single moment to shatter our dreams.

I survey the store, filled with my handmade wooden creations. It had started as a way to keep myself busy after I stopped playing music, but it quickly turned into a passion. People began commissioning pieces from me and before I knew it, woodworking had become my main source of income. Then my dad passed away and everything changed. My mom had wanted to sell the ranch multiple times, even receiving a generous offer once. But the thought of losing this stable childhood home is unbearable to me. I moved back to the ranch and now, I divide my time between hard labor and solitary days and nights in the barn, creating new pieces. Each one holds memories of Bayleigh, which I keep close to my heart.

The images on the woodwork, whether they result from her music playing on the radio or just remind me of that first carving I made her long ago, always bring her to mind. Our bond had been unbreakable, even after we were physically separated. I can't help but wonder if she felt the same way. That undeniable chemistry and connection that we shared had seemed timeless. Although she had moved on with her new life in Nashville, social media made it difficult for me to not keep up with her career. I listened to her first single, watched her make her debut at a big show, and celebrated when she played at the Grand Ole Opry for the first time. Her journey has been like a reality TV show, with all its highs and lows broadcasted for everyone to see. Her name is constantly making headlines in town.

I don't envy her all the publicity; I value my privacy too much. While she is under constant scrutiny, I can do whatever I want without anyone reporting on it. But if we had followed through with our plans for the future, I would have faced the same level of scrutiny she has.

We might have still been together now, enduring everything side by side.

Sometimes I wonder what it would have been like if she hadn't left. If she would have allowed me to be in her life. Maybe she wouldn't have turned to drinking and drugs. Would she have needed to escape the pain? I run my hand through my hair, lost in thoughts of what could have been. But dwelling on the past won't change anything; all I can do is focus on the present. Whatever happened was meant to happen, whether it was part of a greater plan or just random chance.

I pick up the local newspaper that arrived that morning and see a photo on the front page of Bayleigh on stage at Monty's last night. In the picture, I am behind her, playing guitar. I briefly wonder if anyone could tell there was tension between us from watching our performance. Just seeing the picture makes my heart race a little faster.

The headline, printed in big black letters at the top, reads, "Local songstress plays old haunt."

I pull up a stool and sit down to read the article. Might as well torture myself some more.

Grammy-winning country artist Bayleigh Gilmore returned to Sweetgum Valley this week ahead of her upcoming drought-relief charity concert this coming Saturday.

Locals and visiting tourists at Monty's last night were treated to an impromptu performance which reunited the star with her childhood sweetheart and bandmate, Chase Tutton.

Ms. Gilmore, daughter to Marilyn and Paul Gilmore, was born in Sweetgum Valley and attended the local schools until her move to Nashville when she was sixteen years old. The star hasn't been seen in town since, but with such a busy career, who can blame her?

Bayleigh and Chase are reported to have been inseparable in their childhood and were members of a group which performed at open mic nights and other shows.

Mr. Tutton, owner of Tutton Ranch and part owner of Sweetgum Arts & Crafts, is a talented performer in his own right...

I skim to the bottom of the article before crumpling the paper into a ball and tossing it into the garbage bin beneath my desk. I have no interest in reading about my own past, especially not in such a public forum. I can't help but wonder how Bayleigh feels when she reads these types of articles, or if her team even allows her to see them. Thankfully, they haven't mentioned Harper or the real reason Bayleigh left town before graduation. It's surprising that this story hasn't made headlines yet; I've often wondered how she's managed to keep it out of the press for so long. But I have no desire to profit from such a personal experience.

The first two years after Bayleigh left were the most difficult. Every day, I went to school not knowing where she was or if I would ever see her again. I grieved as if she had passed away and accepted that she was gone for good. Her parents told me she didn't want to be found, didn't want anything to do with our town or its people anymore. So, I learned to live without her, but she had always been my guiding light. Without her, I felt lost.

Right before graduation, I saw her name on a poster for a concert in Nashville. I skipped out on the ceremony and went to see her perform.

As I watched her on stage, there was a sadness in her eyes and a rawness in her voice that hadn't been there before. It was then that I realized she was on a different path—one that didn't include me.

So I'd watched her, then left. By the time I'd driven the four hours back to Sweetgum, I'd resolved myself to the idea of living without her. After all, if she wanted me in her life, she knew where I'd be.

And just in case she ever changed her mind, I stayed right here in this town. Exactly where she'd left me.

I look at my watch. I'm not supposed to be here. This is not the day I typically work. My coworker, Janine, called me this morning and asked if we could swap days, as her daughter is sick and needs to stay home from school. Despite having a long list of chores waiting for me, I agreed and made the trip back into town. It's just in my nature to help others when they need it. My mother instilled that in me at a young age.

I can't handle any more emotions or chaos from Bayleigh. She'll be leaving soon enough. Part of me is relieved, but another part is saddened. I can't help but feel drawn to her and want to soak up every moment with her before she's gone for good. But my logical side reminds me to keep my distance and remember that there won't be many more chances to see her before she leaves, possibly never to return again.

CHAPTER SEVEN

ayleigh

THE REST of the weekend flies by. The mayor and I meet and I pose for the promised photo shoot while Kelly puts together the agenda for the rest of the week. That's how I find myself at Sweetgum Valley High School on Monday afternoon.

I peek through the curtains of the school auditorium, my eyes widening as I take in the scene before me. Excited teenagers sit on the floor, squeezed between adults who occupy chairs or stand along the sides of the room, all vying for a good view. Video cameras have been set up on tripods and photographers are perched with their cameras, ready to capture today's performance. The pressure is immense; there is so much riding on Saturday's show and I can't afford to give the press any reason to write negatively about me. These kids and this community look up to me as a role model, and I won't let them see the failures and regrets of my past.

When Kelly first told me about performing at the school, I didn't know what to expect, so I'd spent the morning rehearsing and preparing for anything. The teachers had happily canceled classes for the afternoon just to come watch me sing with the school band. It's a far cry from the shows in my early days of targeting teenage audiences, when I'd sing about kissing boys under the bleachers and going to Dairy Queen. Now, my songs reflect a life I have left behind—one full of long hours, vocal training, and performances that took over my life during what should have been my senior year.

I step back and let the curtain fall into place. I take a deep breath as I remind myself that I can do this. I can perform in front of an audience full of teenagers and their parents, some of whom I may have known in the past.

Could Chase be out there? Maybe he's a father now. He could have a wife and kids, keeping true to the norm in Sweetgum Valley. I didn't see a ring on his finger, but that's not unusual for ranchers. And around here, most people here tend to stay put.

My own parents were third-generation residents of Sweetgum Valley and highly respected members of society. My mother even served on the school committee when I was a student here.

The thought of my mother sends a sharp pain through my heart. I've trained myself not to be affected by mentions of my parents or any other family members. We may share DNA, but they are no longer my family.

"Bayleigh?"

I turn at the sound of a familiar voice and see a slim woman with short brown hair walking towards me with a nervous smile.

"Oh my gosh, Ms. Yates?" Tears well in my eyes as I take in the sight of my old teacher. "You look exactly the same." I open my arms wide for a hug.

"You look amazing." Ms. Yates smiles graciously. "I wasn't sure you would recognize me."

"I will always remember you as my favorite teacher; your music and singing classes helped me get this far."

"You and Chase were both so talented. I've been keeping up with your career, which is why the school band already know all your songs."

I laugh. "Now it makes sense how they were able to perform on such short notice."

Ms. Yates places a comforting hand on my arm. "I am incredibly proud of you and all you've accomplished."

"Thank you." I swallow back the emotions tightening in my throat. Not many people have ever expressed pride in me; usually I'm just a disappointment. But Ms. Yates is different. She had been an ally for Chase, Harper and me in school, helping our band practice and organizing performances and competitions. She believed in us when few others did.

Her voice lowers to a soft tone. "Will you be visiting your mother while you're here?"

I shake my head, my earrings swaying against my cheeks.

"I see her every now and then." Ms. Yates leans in closer, perhaps to avoid being overheard. "She's never been the same since . . . well, you know."

Although my teacher has no intention of causing harm, I can't help feeling guilty. "And what about my dad?"

"He left a long time ago. I have no idea where he is now."

Kelly interrupts us before the news fully sinks in. "We're getting started soon."

"Good luck," Ms. Yates says and squeezes my hand before heading off to join the band.

"Are you ready?" asks the principal, an elderly man with a warm smile.

I nod. "Absolutely." I swallow hard as he walks out onto the stage, and the room falls silent for his introduction.

"We are honored to have a special guest here today. She attended this very school, sang in the choir, and competed in many competitions. Today she will be performing with our school band. Please give a warm welcome to Bayleigh Gilmore!"

The curtains part and I stand center stage in front of a microphone stand with the band behind me. The audience cheers and whistles, and I take a moment to bask in the applause. I place my hand over my heart and smile gratefully. "Thank y'all so much. It's such an honor to be back at my old high school."

Another round of applause fills the auditorium, and I giggle into the microphone. "Thank you, thank you." I turn to face the band, and Ms. Yates stands, ready to conduct. We share a smile before I turn back to address the audience.

"When I went here, I was in a band, Ms. Yates, over here? She was my music teacher, and she helped me so much back then. Y'all are so lucky to have her here, still teaching almost two decades later. Let's give her a round of applause everyone. Ms. Yates!"

I gaze at the eager faces of the young audience members, knowing that with the right mentorship and encouragement, they could achieve anything. I was grateful to have had that kind of support from my teacher and bandmates, especially Chase and Harper. Harper, who had once performed alongside us on this very stage, but never as a student in this high school.

"I used to perform on this stage a lot to my classmates and I always dreamed of performing to crowds of people and doing stadium tours and selling out arenas. I dreamed big, and I worked real hard and I made it." I take the microphone out of the stand and walk toward the front of the stage. "I often get told by people that they want to be like me. Maybe not entirely like me." I chuckle. "Kids, don't do drugs. It's bad!" I say in as joking a tone as I can and hopefully still get my point across. "But y'all don't want to be like me. You want to be you. This is your journey, your life, and you have got to make the most of it. If you want to sing, sing. If you want to write, write. Don't let anyone hold you back from achieving your dreams. Do what makes you light up. Do what you love to do. Be yourself, because you are beautiful. Each and every single one of you."

I turn back to Ms. Yates and nod for her to start. The teen at the keyboard plays the introduction to one of my favorite, empowering songs and I sing it with more heart, hope, and gratitude than I have ever sung with before, and the students sit, looking at me with open mouths and starstruck eyes.

It is impressive how familiar the band is with every beat of the song. For a high school band, they play exceptionally well. But then again, they do have the best teacher, so their talent isn't exactly surprising. We end up playing three songs in total, each one better than the last. As we finish, the audience erupts into applause that can probably be heard down the street. I take a deep bow and waved to the cheering crowd, thanking them for their support before handing the microphone back to the principal and making my way off stage.

"That was amazing," Kelly says, handing me a bottle of water. "I got some great shots for social media." Kelly turns her phone to show me.

"Oh, that one is really good," I say, pointing to the photo of me looking back at the band with a bright smile.

"When you're ready, there will be a meet-and-greet with some parents and students. The band, in particular, would like some photos with you."

I follow Kelly's lead and engage in conversations with the students about their music, interests, and experiences in the industry. I sign autographs, and the students and I take many photos and share plenty of hugs. After that, I greet the adults who are waiting to meet me when I see a familiar face. "Coralee Masters? Is that really you?" I study the woman in front of me.

The woman with short blonde hair smiles back. "I can't believe you remember your old friend; it's been so long."

"How could I forget you!" I hug her and breathe in her fruity scent. "How are you?"

"I'm good. My oldest daughter is in the band. She was so excited to play with you."

"Wow, they were so great. Which one is she?"

Coralee points to her tall, slim daughter with a bouncy high ponytail. "That's Emma. She played violin."

"Yes, I talked to her. She's really good."

Coralee beams at her proudly. "Your success really is inspirational. I'm sure it hasn't always been easy, but you have made a name for yourself. I have all your albums."

"That's so sweet. Thank you." I note the line forming behind her. "It's so great to see you."

"You too, Bayleigh. It's wonderful to see you." Coralee walks away as the next person steps forward to greet me. As I watch her go, a strange thought crosses my mind: if I hadn't left when I did, Coralee's life could have been mine. I could have settled down here, bought a house, and found a job. My children could have attended the same school as I did and joined the same school band. This could have been my life. But it isn't.

For the next hour, I chat with various people, my cheeks hurting from smiling so much. It is a good day though. It makes me appreciate spending time with regular people instead of constantly being surrounded by other musicians and people in the industry. Sometimes I forget my fans are real individuals with their own lives and struggles.

They came out today to support me, and for that, I am incredibly grateful.

* * *

THAT EVENING, the Sweetgum Valley Council hosts a special dinner in my honor. Kelly assists me in selecting an outfit from our shopping trip the day before day. I settle on a sophisticated black cocktail dress with rhinestones and off-the-shoulder sleeves, reaching just above my knees. To complete the look, I wear shiny white cowgirl boots adorned with fringes.

We make our way down to the hotel's grand ballroom, where a swarm of eager press photographers and reporters await us. I put on my best smile and strike a few poses for their cameras before entering the room. The space is filled with people socializing over glasses of champagne, while Kelly, as always, is at my side, introducing me to everyone and keeping the conversation flowing. A waiter hands me a glass of sparkling mineral water with a lemon slice garnish—my new go-to drink to avoid any temptation of alcohol. The photographers are always looking for that "money shot" of me falling off the wagon again, but Kelly is vigilant in making sure no one sabotages her boss's sobriety by accidentally serving alcohol. Maintaining my recovery is tough enough without any external pressure or temptation.

The guests at tonight's event are primarily local businesses and supporters of the upcoming weekend event. I don't recognize most of them, so I assume they must be new to the area. There is a band on the stage singing country music covers and I smile as I think of all the gigs like this I once played.

Eventually, we are asked to take our seats, and appetizers are served. Kelly and I sit with the mayor and many other important figures, making small talk and expressing our gratitude for their generous contributions.

Then, the mayor steps onto the stage and delivers a speech about how this weekend's event will raise funds for the town, particularly considering the recent drought that has devastated local agriculture and businesses. He outlines plans for where the donations will go and how it will help boost community morale.

"We are honored and thrilled to have Bayleigh Gilmore return to our town this week to support our cause, and I would like to bring her up to the stage now to say a few words."

I stand, smooth down my dress, and join the mayor on the stage. He hands me the microphone. Kelly had warned me I would be asked up, so I have already rehearsed for this. I thank the mayor and everyone attending as I look out at the crowd of people who have come together to help my hometown in its time of need.

"Y'all know I'm better at singing than speaking, so how about I do that for y'all tonight?" I ask and am met by a roar of excitement. I turn and nod to the band behind me and start singing one of my songs. As always, I turn inward and put all my focus on my performance, putting my whole heart into the lyrics. This is how I capture the audience's attention.

I lose myself in the music and the lights, and let the song speak for me.

CHAPTER EIGHT

hase

I WATCH her from the shadows at the back of the room, mesmerized by her ability to captivate the audience with every note. This is a talent she has possessed since I first met her. It's what makes her such an incredible performer, and when that's combined with the perfect songs written specifically for her, it is no surprise that she remains one of the greats, despite any past indiscretions.

She looks stunning in her black dress and boots, her blonde curls cascading down her back, a glimmering chain around her neck. Others try to imitate her style, but this is simply a part of who Bayleigh is; there is no need for her to try to be anyone else.

The applause erupts around me as the song comes to an end, snapping me out of my trance. I wave over a waiter and quickly take a sip from the flute they offer me. I'm only here because Frankie begged me to come. He hopes that rubbing elbows at this social event would open up some doors for our band. Right now, he's deep in conversation with Kelly, Bayleigh's assistant, and I can't help but wonder if his intentions tonight are more than just business-focused.

I look towards the door, already planning my escape when Frankie jabs me in the ribs.

My body freezes as Bayleigh gracefully strides over to our group and joins us. She looks breathtaking tonight. And those sparkly boots! I wouldn't mind if she kept them on in the bedroom.

Our eyes meet for a brief moment before she turns and talks to Kelly. I finish my drink and try to focus on what Kelly is saying. She then gestures towards Frankie and me. "Do you remember Frankie, the lead singer from the band who played the other night at Monty's?"

Bayleigh smiles and shakes Frankie's hand. "You were amazing. I'm surprised you haven't been signed yet."

"Thank you so much. That means a lot," Frankie says, but I can't hear their conversation anymore. I'm too consumed by the scent and feel of being near Bayleigh. Her necklace dips into the small space between her breasts, and I wonder if a pendant hangs from it. Something precious she holds close to her heart? Her breasts are full and pale, and I have the urge to feel their weight in my hands. Desire stirs deep within me. I've been with plenty of women over the years. I've dated casually, but I've never found someone who I could see myself in a serious relationship with.

Bayleigh was my first everything: my first friend, my first girlfriend. My first kiss, My first love. The memory of our first time, where we both lost our virginity, often keeps me awake at night. I relive those tender moments of touch and kisses, the rush of sensations and release that only ever felt as good with her. The way she trembled in my arms, her soft gasps, the way our souls seemed to meld into one—it was pure magic. Even now, the mere thought of those nights sends a shiver down my spine, a longing so fierce it aches. She isn't just a part of my past; she is a part of me. And no matter how much time has passed, that connection burns as brightly as ever—a flame that refuses to be extinguished.

"Can you move in closer?" A photographer gestures. I step to the side, knowing I'm not important enough to be included in a picture with Bayleigh Gilmore. But Kelly and Frankie wave me back over, so I oblige.

"Stand here, next to Bayleigh." Kelly shows me where to pose, so I'm flanking Bayleigh with Frankie on the other side.

"A little bit closer," directs the photographer. I take another step closer and stand at a slight angle, with Bayleigh's back against my chest. I breathe in her fragrant scent and try my best to focus as the photo is taken.

I linger in that position just a moment longer than Bayleigh, who turns towards me and accidentally brushes her bare arm against my chest. Our eyes meet and she apologizes reflexively, as one does when touching a stranger by accident. But those are the words I have been longing to hear from her.

I desperately want an apology from her. Something that shows she regrets her actions and the pain she's caused me.

But when our eyes meet, an electric jolt of longing surges through me, leaving me frozen and unable to look away. For a fleeting moment, I let myself drown in the sea of possibilities, hoping that perhaps, against all odds, things could be different between us.

My heart aches, a deep and painful throb as she glances at my mouth, her lips parting slightly as if she has something to say but doesn't know how to say it. Her gaze is searing, a tangible touch that leaves my skin burning and my pulse racing. Every moment feels stretched, and the space between us shrinks as if the world itself is urging us to close the gap.

The emotions that swell within me are a tempest—desire, regret, love, and a desperate yearning for what once was. Her presence is intoxicating, and the memories of our shared past flood my mind, each one more vivid and bittersweet than the last. The connection between us is undeniable, a flame that refuses to be extinguished, burning brightly despite the years and the distance that have separated us.

However, we both know that our lives have taken different paths, and there seems to be no way for them to intersect. But a small part of me still wants to try.

My hand reaches out and touches her arm of its own volition. She tilts her head down to where my hand is resting on her skin, but makes no move to stop me. Slowly, my calloused thumb brushes over her soft, pale bicep.

When she raises her head again, there is a silent plea in her eyes. Reluctantly, I remove my hand. With just one look, I can tell that her feelings for me never truly went away either. The intense connection we once had is still there despite the time and distance that has separated us.

In an effort to keep myself in check, I step back into the shadows. Just because the connection remains doesn't mean it's good for either of us. We lead completely different lives now with no room for compromise.

As I watch Bayleigh being swept away by Kelly to socialize with others, I can't help but hope that she will turn around and look at me one more time.

"Dude, something crazy is going on between you two!" Frankie appears in front of me, blocking my view of Bayleigh.

I clear my throat before replying with a dry tone, "There's some history there."

Frankie grins knowingly and opens his mouth as if to say something.

"Don't even ask," I cut him off before he can start. "I think I'm going to call it a night."

There's a look of disappointment on Frankie's face, but it quickly changes to determination. "Alright, man. Thanks for coming. I know you hate these things." He squeezes my shoulder gently. "Thank you."

"You're welcome." I smile back at him. "Now go get yourself a record deal!"

"I'll do my best." Frankie grins and heads back into the crowd.

I scan the room and easily spot Bayleigh surrounded by fans. I let my gaze linger on her, knowing that this will probably be the last time I see her. She will likely be kept busy and unless she steps into my gallery again, there's no reason for our paths to intersect. I've made peace with leaving the past in the past; there's no sense in digging it up now. Nothing good could come from that.

With one final look at Bayleigh, I turn and make my way towards the exit, ready to return to my quiet life away from the spotlight.

CHAPTER NINE

ayleigh

THE AROMA of freshly brewed coffee fills my senses as I wake up. My night was filled with restlessness, my mind consumed by thoughts of Chase. Whenever he crosses my mind, a sinking sensation drops into my stomach. My therapist would probably label it as regret, but maybe guilt is a more fitting term.

I sit up in bed and rub my tired eyes. I'm itching to start working on some new music. I love performing, but I also love being in the recording studio, creating new sounds.

"Kelly?" I call out, and my faithful assistant appears at the door with a steaming cup of coffee.

"Morning. I had that cute diner down the road deliver this for you."

I wrap my hands around the warm cup and take a deep breath. "Thank you." After taking a sip, I place the cup on the bedside table. "I need some new songs for my next album. Can you have Brendon start looking for some?"

"Already on it." Kelly pulls out her iPad and starts typing furiously. "He's been asking around and should have some options for you soon. I know the album isn't locked in till you've done the show on Saturday, but things are looking good for that—especially after yesterday."

"Great." I push back the covers and stand up next to the bed. "I need this comeback album to be really exceptional."

"Have you ever tried writing your own songs?" Kelly asks with a frown.

I shake my head. "No, not in years! I'm not a songwriter. There are much more talented people out there for that."

"Okay." Kelly shrugs. "I think you could write some amazing songs if you tried."

Before I can reply, Kelly's iPad pings with an incoming email.

Kelly's expression turns somber as she looks up from her iPad, her eyes filled with concern. "That was a message from Brendon," she says gravely, her voice trembling slightly. "Cam, has come down with the flu. He won't be able to play the show."

"Seriously? How will we find a guitarist at such short notice?" I exclaim, collapsing onto the bed in frustration. "What are we going to do?"

Kelly sighs, her shoulders slumping. "Brendon has been reaching out to musicians, but everyone who knows your music is already booked for other gigs."

"Damn," I mutter under my breath, running my hand through my hair in exasperation. The weight of the impending setback presses heavily on my chest. "We can't cancel the show. It's too important."

"I have an idea," Kelly says slowly, moving closer to me on the bed, her eyes filled with determination. "I know you remember Chase from Frankie's band. He played with you guys the other night and he was amazing."

I swallow hard, my heart racing at the thought of reaching out to Chase. "But he doesn't know our set. He might not even be available."

Kelly's eyes narrow with resolve. "There's still time to rehearse with him before the show. It's not for a few days. We have to try."

I wrack my brain for any other option, my mind spinning with anxiety. I don't want to spend more time with Chase than necessary; his presence is like a tempting drink, reminding me of what I can't have. "He'll probably turn us down," I say, my voice tinged with doubt.

"That doesn't mean we shouldn't ask," Kelly insists, her voice steady and encouraging. "We need to give it a shot. He might surprise us."

"Alright," I concede, my heart pounding with a mix of hope and dread. "Ask him for help but continue searching for other options. He can't be our only choice."

Kelly nods, her face a mask of determination as she exits the room to make the call. I watch her go, feeling a surge of gratitude for her unwavering support. Alone in the room, I take a deep breath, trying to steady my nerves. This comeback album means everything to me, and I can't afford any more setbacks.

The idea of reaching out to him fills me with unease. I don't need any more distractions in my life right now and Chase would definitely be a distraction. I collapse onto the bed, letting out a groan. This trip just keeps getting more complicated.

CHAPTER TEN

hase

I STEP out onto the porch of my cottage and close the door behind me. The air is brisk on this early fall morning, a reminder that winter is approaching. This year, it's expected to be warmer than usual, which doesn't bode well for relief from the drought. I pause on the porch, taking in a few deep breaths of the fresh mountain air before admiring the picturesque view. My cottage is situated a short distance away from the main house, separated by hedges and a pebbled path. I built this place in my early twenties after moving back home to give me some privacy from my parents. After my father passed away, my mother offered to switch houses with me and live in the smaller cottage so I could have the larger main house. But I declined; I built my cottage myself and it suits my needs perfectly. It may not be fancy or luxurious, but it's clean and functional—just like me. I've never been one for material possessions, and this small cottage is all I need to feel content.

My mom is outside hanging laundry on the line, and she waves me over with a warm smile. I quickly slip on my worn-out cowboy boots from beside the door. As I walk over to where my mom is working, the familiar scent of fresh linen and the earthy aroma of the garden fill the air. We both wake up early every day to tend to the ranch and do housework, a routine that suits us both perfectly and strengthens our bond.

"Good morning, Mom," I say, reaching her side. Her eyes sparkle with the same kindness and resilience that have always guided our family through thick and thin.

"Good morning, sweetheart," she responds, her hands deftly pinning a shirt to the line. "It's another beautiful day," my mom says with a smile. It's become a bit of an inside joke between us.

"I can't even remember when we last had some rain." I grab a shirt from the laundry basket to help.

We share a moment of quiet understanding, appreciating the simple yet profound connection that comes from working together. It's in these small, shared tasks that our relationship truly thrives, each action a testament to our mutual respect and affection.

"Maybe they'll do a rain dance at the concert."

"It's worth a shot." My mom steps away from the clothesline and places her hands on her hips. "Have you seen her yet?"

I fill my mom in on the meetings with Bayleigh, recounting how difficult it's been to see her again after all these years. My mom listens quietly, her eyes filled with understanding and compassion. She's always had a way of knowing when to offer advice and when to simply lend an ear.

"She seems different now," I continue. "More guarded, but also more determined. It's like she's trying to rebuild herself piece by piece."

My mom nods thoughtfully, hanging the last of the laundry. "People change, especially after going through something traumatic. Maybe this time back home will help her find some peace."

I can't help but feel a pang of nostalgia as I think back to the days when Bayleigh and I were inseparable. Her laughter used to fill these fields; her presence as natural as the changing seasons. But those days are long gone, and the reality of our separate lives is stark and unyielding.

"Do you think she'll stay long? After the concert I mean," my mom asks, breaking the silence.

I shrug, unsure how to answer. "I don't know. Part of me hopes she does, but another part knows it might be best for both of us if she moves on, resumes her life in Nashville."

"She was an important part of your life," my mom

reminds me. "What happened was unfortunate. Her mother has never been able to move past it."

I nod in understanding. Mrs. Gilmore had transitioned from being a respected community member to living in social isolation. Her constant bitterness and sharp words had slowly driven a wedge between her and those who once cared for her.

My mother sighs, giving me a knowing look. "Sometimes facing the past is the only way to truly move forward. Maybe this is Bayleigh's chance to do just that."

I ponder her words as we finish up the morning chores. The sound of a vehicle catches my attention, and Frankie's truck pulls into the gate.

I stride to the driveway and meet him as he parks. Frankie gets out and stands there, that big goofy grin on his face, flanked by Kelly.

Kelly smiles widely. She really is very pretty, and she has that people-pleasing cheerleader vibe about her.

"Morning." I frown, looking back at Frankie. "What's going on?"

"Can we talk?" Kelly asks.

I hesitate for a moment, but my manners take over. "Sure, come on in." I gesture towards my cottage, and we walk over and go inside to the living room.

Kelly and Frankie make themselves comfortable on the couch while I stick my hands in the back pockets of my jeans. "Can I get you guys a drink?"

"No, thanks," Kelly responds before turning to Frankie.

Frankie clears his throat and fixes his gaze on me, excitement dancing in his eyes. "An amazing opportunity has presented itself."

"Oh yeah?" I expect news that Frankie's landed a record deal.

But then Kelly speaks up. "The guitar player who was supposed to play with Bayleigh this weekend fell ill and can't make it. We need a replacement."

"Okay . . ." I narrow my eyes at them suspiciously as they exchange glances before Frankie continues.

"They want you, Chase. After your performance the other night, they were blown away and want you to join Bayleigh's band."

My jaw drops. "Wait, what? Me? You're kidding, right?"

They both shake their heads. Kelly smiles widely. "You are incredibly talented and would be an excellent addition to the show."

"This could mean big things!" Frankie adds.

I shake my head in disbelief. "No way. I'm not a professional musician. Get one of your fancy guitar players to fill in. I'm not cut out for this."

"But you are!" Kelly rises from her seat and comes over to me, placing a hand on my arm. "Bayleigh specifically requested you."

I quickly turn my head to meet her gaze. There is no way she actually wants me to play alongside her on stage. Sure, that one performance we did together was incredible, but it was a one-time thing. She couldn't possibly want me for such a big show. This is supposed to be her big comeback, and I don't want to ruin it for her. There is too much at stake.

"We all heard you at Monty's. The chemistry between you when you played was like nothing I've ever experienced," Kelly explains.

"You have to do this, man. It's a once-in-a-lifetime opportunity that you can't turn down," Frankie adds, coming to stand next to me. "This is a huge deal."

"It is," I reply, my voice louder than I'd intended. "But there are other musicians with more experience who would be better suited for this. I just play for fun; I don't want this kind of pressure."

"We need you, Chase," Kelly pleads. "Bayleigh needs you. And the town needs you."

"Think about Sweetgum Valley and all the families that could benefit from the money this show will bring in," Frankie insists.

"Shit, guys, that's not fair." I run my hand through my hair, feeling overwhelmed. All I want is a simple and quiet life. I'm not the young dreamer who craved fame and bright lights anymore. I have already lost my chance once before, and I don't want it again.

"Just come to one rehearsal and see how it goes," Kelly urges me. "If you hate it, we'll find someone else. Please?"

I take a deep breath and look at both Kelly and

Frankie before spotting my guitar in its stand by the TV. A wave of anticipation washes over me as memories flood back: cheering crowds, bright stage lights, and the steady beat of the drums. "Fine. One rehearsal, but no promises."

"Yes!" Frankie punches the air in excitement. "You won't regret this."

"Why do you even care? It should be you up there," I say.

"Nah, I'm a singer, not a guitarist," Frankie replies with a shrug. "But having you on stage will only make us look better as a band."

Kelly nods in agreement. "The record label is very interested in signing your guys."

"As I told Frankie, I'm not looking to change careers now. I'll help the guys out, but don't include me in any big plans. Music is just a hobby now. I'm not trying to make it anything more than that."

Kelly's smile tightens, and she nods again, clearly holding back any further arguments. "I'll forward you the setlist so you can practice today and then come in for rehearsal tomorrow at nine am. I'll text you the details."

"Fine." I open the door for them and watch as they walk down the path together, with Frankie draping his arm around Kelly's shoulders.

I shake my head in disbelief. Something is definitely blossoming between those two.

As I shut the door and lean against it, my gaze falls

back to my guitar. What were they thinking, asking me? Whose stupid idea was this, anyway? Can't have been Bayleigh's, surely.

After she left town, I stayed behind and pieced my life back together, creating a new path for myself that was far different from what we had planned together. We were supposed to share the spotlight and chase our dreams together, but that didn't happen. And now, I doubt she will want to share the stage with me again.

I guess I'll find out for sure tomorrow at rehearsal. I'll keep my word and show up; after all, I'm not the one who breaks promises.

CHAPTER ELEVEN

ayleigh

I OPEN my hotel room door and spot Max standing guard. "Have you seen my assistant?"

"No, ma'am." He shakes his head, then resumes his stance.

I throw my hands up in frustration. Where could Kelly be? It's been forty minutes since she left to check on the band and she still hasn't returned. My nerves are on edge at just the thought of being near Chase again, let alone performing with him. Being on stage together is such an intimate experience for musicians. Performing at Monty's had brought back countless memories and emotions from our past performances at school, shows, and events. We were teenagers then, with big dreams of fame and stardom. I never gave up on those ambitions, and now they're at risk if I can't make this work with Chase. My future depends on it.

Determined not to let this opportunity slip away because of a sick guitar player, I grab my hotel key and head out the door, Max following closely behind. As we wait for the elevator, I can feel the weight of the situation resting heavily on my shoulders. When the doors finally open, I step inside and press the button for the ground floor.

Thankfully, the hotel ballroom has been set up for rehearsals, so I don't have to worry about finding my way to the venue. Things like that are always Kelly's responsibility; she takes care of all the details so I can focus on what I do best. As I step out of the elevator and into the foyer, I scan the room for any signs or landmarks that will lead me to the ballroom, where we need to be.

The floor is empty, but the sound of drums can be heard. I follow the sound until I reach a door. I open it and look inside. The passageway seems familiar. "I know my way from here," I tell Max, who stays behind as I walk down the passage towards the drumbeat.

A slight movement catches my attention, and I pause to get a better look in the dim light. Against a wall of stacked chairs, there is definitely some kind of activity happening. Creeping closer, I can make out two figures—one sitting on a chair, the other astride them. As they move in rhythm, I suddenly realize what is going on.

Kelly, with her long blonde hair flowing wildly, is naked above the waist and has her skirt hiked up around her hips and is riding the man beneath her with fervor. It is a sight that both shocks and arouses me. Unable to tear my eyes away, I watch as her smooth back arches and her perfect breasts bounce against the man's face. A face that I recognize as Frankie's.

My body floods with heat and desire. Moving into the shadows for a better view, I can't help but feel excited by watching Kelly's passionate display. After all, we are all adults here—why not indulge in some harmless voyeurism? As Frankie groans in pleasure and Kelly continues to ride him with abandon, I know this is a memory I will never forget.

Kelly grabs his face and presses her mouth against his as she slows, her bouncing to a gentle rocking motion. His hands reach around to massage her bottom, squeezing and separating her cheeks, giving me an unobstructed view of their joined bodies.

I bite my tongue and squeeze my legs together, trying to contain the urges that arise from watching Frankie move his finger towards Kelly's tight brown asshole. She lets out a cry of pleasure that reaches my ears, despite the loud music in the background. I resist the temptation to touch myself, even though I really, really want to.

I inch closer, wanting a better view of Frankie's finger as he slowly starts to dip it into Kelly's asshole.

"Fuck yes!" Kelly tilts her hips, allowing his finger deeper access into her back passage. His middle finger is now two knuckles deep while his cock is fully enclosed inside her.

Feeling the wetness spreading in my underwear, I finally give in to my urge and lift up my skirt. Crouching in the darkness, I use my fingers to pleasure my clit, the slick juices dripping down my thighs as I watch my assistant being taken by this man in every way imaginable. With a finger in her ass, his cock in her pussy, and their tongues entwined in a passionate kiss, their movements become faster and more urgent until she jerks against him with a muffled cry. Her face flushes red and her body goes limp from the intense fucking she has just received. Frankie's legs tremble as he finishes inside of her and removes his finger from her body, holding her close to him. I bite down on my forearm as I bring myself to climax, my legs shaking and the rest of my body throbbing with pleasure.

After taking a moment to catch my breath, I fix my soaked panties and try to readjust myself. The cool dampness against my sensitive area makes me squirm; I'll be constantly reminded of this experience throughout the day. After standing, I quietly slip back into the hallway. Ensuring I don't disturb the couple lost in their passion, I make my way towards the exit sign above the double doors. The drums continue their rhythmic beat, and I place my palms against my warm cheeks to calm myself down.

I have work to do. Though how I am going to get those images out of my mind, I have no idea.

CHAPTER TWELVE

hase

THE BAND and I have been rehearsing for thirty minutes when Bayleigh finally arrives. Her cheeks are rosy, and I wonder if she took the stairs instead of the elevator. However, a glance at her light blue boots with high heels confirms that likely wasn't the case.

"Hi y'all." She smiles at her bandmates as she strides over to center stage where her mic is waiting in its stand. She takes it in her hand and turns to face me. "Thanks for doing this. We were in a bit of a bind."

"No worries," I reply, then look to Cassie, the brunette, twenty-something drummer who has taken over as the bandleader since the departure of their guitar player. "Cassie has brought me up to speed with the set list."

"Alright, let's start from the beginning." Bayleigh looks around at the rest of the band members. Along with me on acoustic guitar, there is Luke, the bass player, Andy, the electric guitar player, and another woman on keyboard and backing vocals. I am impressed by the talent on stage, but also a bit nervous about my own abilities. These are professional musicians with years of experience and I am such a novice in comparison.

Cassie counts us in and I glance at the sheet music on the floor in front of me, although I don't really need it.

I strum a few chords before Bayleigh stops us.

"No, no, no. It's too slow. Let's speed it up a bit."

The band follows her direction, but she still doesn't seem satisfied after a few more attempts. By the fourth try, I drop my hands from my guitar and let it hang by its shoulder strap. Seriously? What is she hearing? We are playing exactly as she has requested.

Feeling a mix of frustration and resignation, I tighten my grip on the guitar strap as Bayleigh, once again, signals for us to stop mid-song. The tension in the room is palpable, the air thick with unspoken words and mounting irritation. I exchange glances with the other band members; their faces mirror my own exasperation.

Cassie, who I've gathered is the mediator, steps

down from her drum kit and strides over to Bayleigh. Their conversation is hushed, but the animated gestures and furrowed brows speak volumes. I can't help but feel a pang of annoyance as I watch them. This was supposed to be a simple rehearsal, but it has turned into a critique session.

I approach Andy, the electric guitar player, my steps heavy with the weight of my growing discontent. "Do you have any idea what's going on?" I ask, my tone betraying my weariness.

Andy shrugs his shoulders, his expression one of resigned amusement. "She can be a bit of a diva. Especially with this show being so important. We just have to be patient and do what she says. But hey, I'm getting paid by the hour, so it's fine by me."

Cassie breaks away from Bayleigh and gives me a thumbs-up when Bayleigh isn't looking. I give her a questioning look, but she shakes her head slightly in response.

During the next run-through, we manage to play more than half the song before Bayleigh stops us. But after three hours, I am exhausted and my fingers are throbbing. My patience is wearing thin.

Bayleigh turns to me with an accusatory stare and yells, "It's G, not C. Why can't you play it right?"

Everyone falls silent.

I look at my sheet music to confirm that I was playing the correct chord. A wave of indignation surges through me as I look back at her. Enough is enough. I take my guitar off my shoulder, my hands trembling with frustration, and give her a stern look. "I told them from the start that I wasn't the right person for this. I said I would give it a shot, and I did. Now, I quit." With that, I spin on my heel, grab my things, and start walking down the aisle towards the exit, my steps echoing my resolve.

"Wait, Chase." Kelly catches up to me as I reach the exit. "Please stay. She's just in a mood. I'll talk to her."

I look over her shoulder to see Bayleigh talking to Andy and Luke, and doesn't seem all that worried about my exit. Probably happy that she won't have to deal with me anymore.

"No thanks. Nothing is worth putting up with that kind of treatment," I say firmly before pushing through the door, down the hall, and out of the building.

I find my car and sit in the driver's seat. I take a moment to catch my breath. Did I really just walk out of there? I always knew show business could be tough. Maybe if this had happened earlier in my career, I would have had more patience for it. But not anymore. I am done being taken for granted.

If Bayleigh wants a new guitar player, she can find someone else. It certainly won't be me anymore.

CHAPTER THIRTEEN

I AM both glad and upset at the same time, an unfamiliar mix of emotions for me. I never expected Chase to walk out on me. People don't usually question me; they just do what I ask. But Chase doesn't seem to understand this dynamic, and it frustrates me. This concert is a crucial moment for my career, and if it fails, there will be no comeback album, no tour, nothing. I can't afford to fade into obscurity at this point in my life. I need this to work. Deep down, I know that Chase is good, and he was right about that note. My frustration towards him is probably due to a combination of factors: the stress of the show, being in this town, and seeing Kelly getting intimate with Frankie earlier.

The truth is, Chase is more than good—he has mastered all of my songs with such passion and precision that it is as if he has been playing them for years, feeling every note as deeply as I do. It is awe-inspiring, and I can't deny that it stirs something within me— something I haven't felt in a long time. While I freshen up in the bathroom, I let myself get lost in a whirlwind of emotions, imagining Chase dedicating himself to learning my songs, listening to them over and over, absorbing every nuance until he could play them with the kind of heart and soul that only he possesses.

At sixteen, he had set the bar high. He was not only my first sexual partner, but also my best one to this day. The connection we shared was electric, a blend of innocent curiosity and raw passion. I can still recall the way his touch sent shivers down my spine and his eyes bored into mine, filled with a mix of wonder and intensity.

However, I can't help but wonder if my memories are accurate after all these years. Time has a way of altering perceptions, and perhaps I've romanticized those moments. But the truth remains that being with Chase was extraordinary, something that transcended the physical act itself. The way he made me feel cherished and understood is unparalleled.

Has he pleased countless women since me? Maybe he is even married with a big family, but I never bothered to ask. I don't want to know the reality; my fantasy memory is probably better, anyway. Yet the thought of him with someone else gnaws at me, a bitter pang of jealousy mixing with the nostalgia.

I can still picture the way his fingers danced on the guitar strings, the same way they once traced patterns on my skin. His eyes, deep and soulful, seemed to hold secrets and emotions that were only shared with me during those intimate moments. The warmth of his embrace, the softness of his whispers in the dark, and the electric connection between us—I can feel them all as vividly as if they had happened just yesterday.

But reality has a cruel way of intruding on my memories. The Chase I knew then and the Chase I've encountered now are worlds apart. He has grown, not just in talent but in stature, carrying himself with a confidence that is both intimidating and alluring. He isn't the man he was. And I sure as hell am not the girl I was back then. Too much has changed.

Yet I can't ignore the lingering feelings. There is an undeniable chemistry, a magnetic pull that draws me to him despite the circumstances. The tension between us is palpable, charged with unresolved emotions and unspoken words.

I make my way back to the stage where Kelly is waiting with her iPad.

"Yeah, I know." I raise my hands in surrender. "We can't have a show without him. Offer him whatever it takes to get him back."

Kelly lets out a shrill laugh. "It's going to take more than money. Chase isn't motivated by that. As you may have noticed, he's already quite successful on his own. This is about pride now."

I drop my shoulders in defeat. "What do you mean?"

"You need to fix things yourself. Did you hear him? He sounded amazing, and so did you all together. You have to find him and beg him to come back, or else we might as well pack up and go home right now. And then we'll have a breach of contract and another lawsuit on our hands."

"Great way to break the news gently, Kelly." I rub my forehead, a headache coming on. "So what should I do?"

"I'll arrange a meeting at a diner—that one with the good coffee we went to before." Kelly quickly types something into her iPad. "You need to swallow your pride and grovel to that man."

"Fuck." I let out a sigh. "Fine, set it up. Today, if possible. We're running out of time. There's only three days till curtains up, and I need to get Chase back on the team. We can't perform without a guitar player. "

"Already on it." Kelly taps her screen. "Now get back to rehearsal."

* * *

KELLY and I arrive at the diner, which is mercifully quiet since I really don't want an audience watching or filming me groveling, if need be, to Chase. He's not there yet, so we sit down and wait. He's late. I glance at the antique analogue clock on the wall and see that he is five minutes behind schedule. I can't shake off the feeling that maybe he's not going to show up or that this is all some ploy to embarrass me. What will I do if he refuses to play at the show? Anxious thoughts race through my mind as I drum my nails on the table.

"You're sure he agreed to meet here?" I ask Kelly.

She nods reassuringly. "He's probably just running behind. You know how things move slower in small towns."

"I have a lot to do this evening, so if he's not here in five . . ." I start to say before Kelly waves at someone behind me and Chase appears, casting a tall shadow over me. My nerves twist in my stomach as Kelly stands and gestures for Chase to take her seat across from me.

"Thank you for coming," she says before moving away to a nearby table, giving me a supportive look. Chase raises his eyebrows at me but remains standing, forcing me to strain my neck to make eye contact with him.

"Please sit down," I say with a shaky breath. He sighs and settles into the chair, crossing his muscular arms over his chest and leaning back. The manual labor of working his ranch has chiseled his biceps, which now strains against his denim shirt. My eyes are drawn to his left hand, the one that controls guitar notes and knows how to create beautiful music. The sight of it makes me flush with desire and remember our previous encounters, where he made me moan and writhe under his touch.

I inhale deeply and meet his gaze, only to see a spark in his eye that makes me think he's been reading my mind and knows exactly what I've been daydreaming about. As if being turned on earlier wasn't enough, now I have even more fantasies to add to my mental spank bank. Might as well just get this over with. "Look, I'm sorry about this morning. You didn't do anything wrong. I'm just stressed and took it out on you," I say in a low voice, feeling like I'm groveling.

He holds my gaze before slowly uncrossing his arms and leaning forward, resting them on the table. His face is close to mine now. "So you're admitting that you were wrong, and I was right?"

My heart races at his slight taunting tone, but I know he's just trying to make me squirm.

"Yes, fine. You were right," I say through gritted teeth, not wanting the whole world to hear me admit it.

A satisfied smile curves across Chase's lips, and the skin at the corner of his eyes crinkles. I remember this look. That mischievous grin.

"What exactly has you so frustrated, Bayleigh?"

"You know what. My career is in the toilet, and if this show isn't a huge success, then I have nothing. No career, no representation, and no future." This time, I cross my arms under my breasts and lean back in the chair. Glancing down, I realize that this has caused my already tight T-shirt to strain even more. The V-neckline is stretching, the white fabric revealing more skin than is appropriate for any daytime business meeting.

Chase's eyes wander down to my chest, and my breath catches in my throat. My heart races as blood rushes towards my lower half. The desire for his touch, for his lips and tongue, becomes almost unbearable. I can't help but wonder if he would be up for a little afternoon delight.

No, stop it. We both know this can't just be a casual fling. Our history is too complicated. It's best to keep things professional and distant.

I slowly uncross my arms and silently urge him to look back at my face. "Please reconsider and perform the show with me," I plead with him. I hate feeling vulnerable like this. It never ends well—just in heartbreak and embarrassment.

He looks at me, all playfulness gone from his expression now. "I understand how important this is to you. This town and these people mean something to me, too. I want this show to be a success." He rubs the back of his neck, looking slightly uncomfortable. "But will you promise to stop being such a diva and trust in the music? It's already great—the band is talented, and they know what they're doing. The more you stress, the worse it gets."

Then he does something that nearly stops my heart.

He reaches out and places his hand on top of mine.

"Remember why we loved performing?" He lowers his head, gazing up at me through those long lashes of his. "Because we loved that connection with the audience. When you relax and enjoy yourself, that connection is strongest."

My throat tightens as I swallow hard. He's right. I've been so focused on every little detail that I haven't been able to let go and just connect with the song. That's when I'm truly authentic—when the music flows through me.

"Do you ever miss those old days? Performing at shows around town?" I ask, a flood of fond memories rushing through my mind.

His fingers gently stroke my skin, sending shivers down my spine. "Yes," he says quietly, holding my gaze with his intense eyes. "I think about you all the time."

My eyes widen at his confession. He pulls his hand back and quickly tucks it under the table. His posture straightens, and an awkward silence falls between us.

I grab the glass of water in front of me and take a long sip as Kelly waves, signaling for me to wrap up the conversation.

Enough of this painful trip down Memory Lane. "So, will you come back to rehearsal?" I ask, trying to sound casual.

Chase nods slowly. "Fine. I'll give you one more chance. Don't screw it up, or I'm out for good."

"Thank you." I let out a sigh of relief. "Do you need to get your guitar? The band is waiting for us."

"It's in my car." He says.

"Let's go then—we don't have much time." I get up from my chair and head towards the exit.

A woman enters the diner. I tense as recognition sets in. It's my mother, but she doesn't look like the woman I remember from my childhood. Her hair is disheveled and grey, and her clothes seem thrown together without any care. Without the style and pride in her appearance, she used to have. We lock eyes from across the room, and it seems we're both afraid to make a move.

The last time we saw each other was in a heated argument filled with tears and screams. Before I stormed out of the house, my mother said something that still haunts me: "You should have been the one to die. Not her!"

As Chase takes hold of my hand, his warm fingers intertwining with mine, he must notice the tension between my mother and me. He asks if I want to talk to her, but I rush to shake my head—I never want to speak to her again.

She breaks our gaze, turns, and hurries out of the diner without a word. I am left looking at the door swinging shut behind her.

My mother hasn't spoken to me in eighteen years. She hasn't even made an effort to contact me.

"Your leaving must have been hard on her," Chase

says quietly. I know he is trying to comfort me, but he doesn't know what really happened between us.

I look at him and try not to let the pain show on my face. "I did what she told me to do," I say. I don't want to talk about it. I've talked with therapists and doctors over the years and rehashing the past has never helped me before.

Chase tries to apologize, but I put my hand up to stop him. I don't want his pity.

"Let's go," I say to Kelly, my voice trembling with a mix of anger and sadness. As we make our way out of the diner, my steps feel heavy, each one echoing the weight of my unresolved pain.

We walk back to the hotel, stopping briefly so Chase can get his guitar. The walk is silent, a palpable tension filling the air as I try to swallow down the emotions bubbling inside me.

Memories of that fateful day rush back, my mother's harsh words ringing in my ears, the heartache of her rejection cutting deeper than any physical wound. I clench my fists, my nails digging into my palms as if the pain could ground me, keep me from falling apart. Chase's presence beside me is a bittersweet comfort; his support is a lifeline, yet it also reminds me of the fragility of human connection and the scars others can leave.

By the time we reach the hotel, I am exhausted, both physically and emotionally. I glance at Chase, whose concerned eyes meet mine, and for a moment, I let my guard down. "Thank you," I whisper, my voice barely audible. It's all I can manage, but he nods, hopefully understanding more than words could convey.

"I just need a minute," I say to Kelly before heading to the bathroom. I lean over the sink and let the silence envelop me, a stark contrast to the chaos within. I know I have to face my past, but for now, I just need to breathe.

CHAPTER FOURTEEN

hase

WE GET INTO A GOOD RHYTHM, and practice goes smoothly for the rest of the afternoon. Bayleigh has been acting a bit distant since her encounter with her mother, but I don't blame her. I can only imagine what it must be like for her to be back here. Especially now I know more about why she left. I want her to tell me the whole story, but I don't want her to feel pressured into telling me. If she wants to she can.

The days after the accident were rough. Everyone was in shock. Bayleigh and I both had bruises from our seat belts and a few minor scrapes. We owe our lives to those safety devices.

I don't remember when Harper took hers off. She

had been fiddling with the radio, leaning over from the backseat and accidentally elbowing me and Bayleigh in her attempt to adjust it. We were all on such a high after winning the battle of the bands, and we'd thought our careers were about to take off after such an amazing performance.

We were exhausted. We had left early that morning to drive to the event, then practiced and prepared all day, and we were less than half an hour away from home. The roads were dark and unfamiliar and winding.

If I could go back in time and insist on driving the car home, I would. I had driven us that route earlier in the day so I was more familiar with the road than Bayleigh was. But it was her car, and she felt responsible for it.

Maybe if I had been driving, Bayleigh would have been the one turning up the volume, and Harper would have stayed safely in the backseat with her seat belt on.

The day of the funeral was the last time I saw Bayleigh. Her face was swollen from crying and her hair was pulled back carelessly. As we stood together at the cemetery, watching as they lowered the casket into the ground, I reached for her hand. She didn't pull away, but she also didn't respond. Her hand felt cold and lifeless in mine as she stared ahead with a blank expression. While everyone else began to leave, Bayleigh stayed rooted in place. Finally, after a long time staring at the freshly dug mound, she allowed me to gently guide her to the car where her parents were waiting to help her inside. She didn't even acknowledge my presence as I shut the door behind her.

I had no idea that would be the last time I saw her.

I always assumed that Bayleigh made the choice to leave because she couldn't bear it any longer. I was there with her in the hospital when her parents were told about Harper's death. Her mother had turned to Bayleigh with venom in her eyes and said, "You did this."

I'd thought that was just a momentary outburst, something she'd said in grief. I believed that they would come together as a family and heal from this tragedy. They'd always been so close before. But without Harper, everything fell apart.

My heart aches for Bayleigh. I can't imagine what she's still going through.

Losing Harper felt like losing a sister to me too. She always had a bright smile on her face and never failed to make us all laugh at her jokes. Just like her sister, she could light up any room she walked into. It was devastating that someone so young and full of potential was taken away.

"Chase." Bayleigh's voice breaks me out of my thoughts, and I turn to look at her.

"Cam and I were going to do an acoustic set of 'Summer Rain' here. Do you want to give it a try?"

I look between the other members, waiting to hear

their thoughts. Do they want me to step up and do it with her? Do they think I should? Am I good enough?

"Go on," Andy says. "It's not any harder than anything else you've done."

"Yeah, okay," I say and flip the sheet music on the floor until I find the right page. I look through it quickly, refreshing my memory. I haven't played this song in a long time.

"Stand over here next to me," Bayleigh says as she removes the mic from the stand.

She counts me in, and I strum the opening chords before she joins me. It feels like old times, just the two of us making music together. I steal a glance at her, and my heart skips a beat. We finish the song and our bandmates clap in approval.

"I messed up a few times. Can we run it again?" I ask, wanting to make it perfect for her.

"Sure." She turns to our bandmates. "Y'all can call it a night. We'll practice this some more. See you tomorrow."

They all say goodnight and leave and then it's just the two of us on stage.

"I think we should sit on stools for this one. What do you think?" she suggests.

"Whatever you want," I reply, grabbing two stools from side stage and bringing them over.

Sitting so closely next to each other on stage feels intimate. We play through the song a few more times, growing better with each rendition until she finally smiles at me. "That was really good."

"It was, yeah." I smile back at her, seeing a glimpse of the young Bayleigh peeking out from behind her solidly built up walls.

"This has always been one of my favorites," she says. "It was written just for me."

"It's perfect for you. It really showcases your voice," I agree. "Do you still write?"

I immediately regret asking because her eyes darken and it's as though her walls go right back up.

She shakes her head. "I don't do that anymore."

"What about that song we wrote? What was it called?" I scratch my chin, lost in the memory of us sitting on her front porch, making up lyrics.

"I can't remember. It was a long time ago." She stands and puts her microphone back in its stand.

I can tell I've hit a nerve, and I don't want to upset her. Glancing at my phone, I say, "It's almost eight. Are you hungry? Want to grab some dinner?"

She looks at me, perhaps thinking for a moment. "Kelly usually takes care of meals. I don't know where she is."

"Probably off with Frankie." I chuckle. "Looks like they've hit it off."

A huge grin spreads across her face. "Yes, they definitely have."

I narrow my eyes at her. "What do you know?"

She pauses before leaning in closer to me. "I saw them together this morning."

Confused, I frown.

She continues, in a quiet voice, "They were having sex in the back room."

My jaw drops. "What? Did you interrupt them?"

She giggles, and that beautiful sound fills the air around us. "No, they didn't see me. But I saw them."

We both laugh together and I imagine her watching from the shadows as they touched, kissed, and fucked hard.

"At least someone's getting some!" She laughs. Before I can come up with a response, she gestures towards the exit. "Come on, let's eat."

"Yep, I'm starving," I agree as we walk off stage.

But now I am hungry for more than just food. I wonder what she did when she saw them. Did she watch? Did she fantasize about it being her? My cock twitches, and I tell myself to stop thinking about it. This is not the time or place for those thoughts. I'll save them for later when I'm alone in bed, wishing she was with me.

ayleigh

CHASE LEADS the way out of the hotel and down the street. I suggest waiting for a taxi, but he insists that the restaurant he wants to take me is within walking distance. I glance back and see Max following a few paces behind us.

The air is chilly out tonight, and I'm grateful for my jumper keeping me warm.

"Where are you taking me?" I ask as we stroll along the empty road.

"You'll see," he says with a grin. "Please tell me you didn't go vegan living in Nashville."

I chuckle. "I tried to for a time but missed red meat too much."

"Good," he says and stops to open a door, waving me inside.

I look up to read the sign. "Barbeque? Really?"

"I bet it's even better than anything you've tried in Nashville."

I laugh. "That's a pretty high bar to beat. But I'm game. You know I love my barbeque."

"Oh, I remember," he whispers as I move past him.

The restaurant smells of cooking meat and sauce, and my mouth waters.

We grab a booth at the back of the nearly empty restaurant and order iced tea.

"You can have a beer if you like," I say to him, but he shakes his head.

"Tea is fine."

"Does your mom still do Sunday barbeque?" I ask.

"Once a month after church. They just keep getting bigger and bigger. Everyone knows they're welcome to come join us."

"That's so generous of her. It must cost a fortune."

He shrugs. "Most people bring sides. There's always a lot of corn, macaroni and cheese, and coleslaw. There are so many people who come not just for the food, which is probably the best meal they have all month because of the drought, but also for the community and fellowship."

"How is the ranch going?" I spent a lot of my days at his family's property when I was young, riding horses and helping out. Our house was in town, but I grew up as a cowgirl because of my time spent at Chase's ranch.

He rests his elbows on the table and speaks softly. "Since my dad passed, it's been up to me to keep it running."

Guilt hits me at the mention of Chase's father passing away. "Oh Chase, I'm so sorry. I didn't know at the time about your dad."

He gives a small nod. "It was a few years ago now. Heart attack. It was sudden."

"That must have been so hard," I say softly. "Your dad was always so kind to me."

Chase nods, a sad smile crossing his face. "He thought the world of you, Bay. Always said you were going places." Chase looks down at the table. "He was disappointed when you left town. We all were."

The use of my old nickname sends a shiver down my spine. No one has called me "Bay" in years. It feels both familiar and strange at the same time.

"I should have known. I should have come back for the funeral," I say quietly, guilt washing over me. "I should have been there for you and your family."

Chase shakes his head. "It's okay. I understand now more about why you stayed away. Things were . . . complicated."

An awkward silence falls between us. There's so much left unsaid, so many years of distance and pain.

The waitress arrives with our drinks, giving us a welcome interruption. As she walks away, I take a long sip of my tea, savoring the familiar taste that brings back memories of summer afternoons on Chase's front porch.

"Everything looks so good," I say as I look over the menu. "I want it all."

"Let's get a bit of everything, then." He flags the waitress over and gives our order. She nods and offers him a friendly smile, then turns to me and takes my menu. She doesn't even flinch with recognition. She doesn't seem to recognize me like most people. It's nice to have some anonymity for a change.

"So what's Nashville like?" He asks.

"Busy but beautiful. It's a great city. Have you ever been?"

He takes a moment to respond, then says, "No, I haven't had much opportunity to travel."

We each take a sip of our drinks. "So woodworking, huh? I remember you and your dad would sit on the porch and whittle things."

"Yeah, it was our thing to do together. Then I took woodwork at school and just kept going from there." He explains.

I listen attentively, happy that he has found something he is passionate about. Sometimes I feel guilty for pushing him to join my band when we were teenagers, but he never complained. He seemed to genuinely enjoy it; his natural talent as a musician is a rare gift. Now, Frankie and his friends are the lucky recipients of it.

"I'm glad you still make time to play guitar," I say.

"Lucky for you, I guess." He grins mischievously, and I am relieved that any awkwardness between us has dissipated. Perhaps it disappeared during rehearsal earlier today—music has a way of breaking down barriers and bringing people together.

"It's a huge help, thank you. And don't worry—I'll make sure you are fairly compensated."

"I'm doing it for the community, so instead of paying me, donate the money to them. They need it more than I do. I make enough from my business to get by." His generosity and sincerity strike me once again; I had almost forgotten this about him.

Our food arrives, and a wide variety of plates are placed in front of us. A tower of steaming ribs is surrounded by sides like beans, coleslaw, and cornbread.

"I hope you have a big appetite," he says with a smile as he offers me a plate of saucy pork ribs, the house specialty.

I take the plate and serve myself a generous portion. Then, with dramatic flair, I roll up my sleeves, grab a rib with both hands, and enjoy a satisfying bite. The flavor is so divine that I can't help but let out a moan before setting the rib back on the plate and reaching for a napkin to clean up any sauce that may have escaped onto my face. I resist the urge to lick my fingers clean, trying to maintain some level of etiquette.

"You like it?" He's been watching me and hasn't touched his food yet. My cheeks heat, and I worry I missed some sauce.

"It's so good. Messy to eat, but the best ribs I've had in a long time." I reach across the table to get the cornbread—one of my all-time favorite foods—and his eyes drift to my uncovered forearm.

"Bay," he says my name with a worried sigh. *He's seen the scar on my wrist.* I withdraw my hand, put the plate down, and quickly roll my sleeve back in place. "Please just forget about it."

His voice is soft and warm. "Bay, what happened to you?"

I look up at him and see something on his face that I haven't seen in years—genuine concern. He's not worried how the scars will affect his career, or his status in the industry. He genuinely is worried about me.

Which means he must still care.

I wipe my hands with the napkin. "Please don't tell anyone. I can't afford any more bad press."

"I'd never say a word. I promise," he says, and his eyes are so gentle.

I bite my bottom lip, considering my next words carefully. "Things have been tough since I left. I've had to do things I'm not proud of—things I regret." My voice falters as memories flood back. "I turned to drugs and alcohol to numb the pain, and there were times when I even tried to end it all." Taking a deep breath, I continue. "But that's all in the past now. I'm looking ahead and determined to make the most out of what's left of my time on this Earth."

We sit in silence for a moment as I hold his gaze. It's hard for me to be vulnerable like this, but with Chase, I feel safe. Trusting people has never been easy for me, but with him, it comes naturally.

"I'm sorry you had to go through that," he says gently, cleaning his hands before reaching over with his palm facing up. Hesitantly, I place my hand in his. He wraps his fingers around mine and gives a reassuring squeeze. Tears threaten to spill from my eyes, but I fight them back. "I'm here now," he says simply, but his words mean everything.

Sniffing, I force a smile. "Come on. Let's not let this delicious food go to waste."

A grin spreads across his face. "Now that would be a tragedy."

We eat and talk and share stories. It is the best meal and the best company I could ask for, and I never want it to end. At this moment, surrounded by good food and great company, I feel at peace. And I never want to lose this feeling again.

CHAPTER SIXTEEN

hase

MY EYES REMAIN LOCKED on Bayleigh as she savors the food before us. She seems so relaxed, a beautiful reminder of the carefree girl she once was. Back then, she didn't care about anyone else's opinions and wouldn't hesitate to lick sauce off her chin with a playful grin. She's more reserved now, but every now and then, a glimpse of my old friend shines through in her cheeky smile.

I steer the conversation towards lighter topics, asking about her tours and encounters with other musicians. She even tells me about some behind-the-scenes moments from the Country Music Awards.

As the waitress clears away the empty plates,

Bayleigh flashes her a grateful smile. The waitress offers us dessert options, mentioning that there are a couple slices of pecan pie left.

Bayleigh and I exchange glances before both eagerly agreeing to order a slice with ice cream.

"Do you remember when we snuck into your mom's kitchen and devoured an entire pecan pie?" Bayleigh chuckles.

I can't help but grin at the mischief we got into. "It was the day before Thanksgiving. We took it to the barn and ate it with our bare hands."

"Because we forgot to take utensils, too."

"We made such a mess."

"But it was worth it." She sinks back against the cushy booth. "I've missed this."

I take a moment to observe her content state before admitting, "I've missed you."

Our eyes meet, and we hold each other's gaze for what feels like an eternity. Unspoken thoughts and emotions fill the space between us. I wonder about what could have been.

The waitress returns with two generous pieces of pecan pie, glossy ice cream scooped in a perfect curve on the side. "Enjoy," she says before leaving.

"This looks incredible. I'm so full from the ribs, but I can't resist!" She moans, leaning in and picking up her fork. She takes a bite, clearly savoring the sugary treat and closing her eyes in delight.

I can't help but remember the blissful expression on

her face when we were together in the barn. The memory of being inside her, pleasuring her and feeling her unravel beneath me. I ache to be with her again. To take her body and remind her how good we are together. I squirm in my seat.

"Are you okay?" Bayleigh asks.

"Yeah, I'm fine," I reply, although my cock is begging for release.

I take a bite of my own dessert, letting the cold ice cream melt in my mouth. It's delicious, but I can't help but imagine tasting her instead, feeling her warm juices on my tongue.

I swallow hard and put my fork down.

"Can I ask you something?" Bayleigh looks at me through her thick lashes.

"Of course," I say.

"What was it like here after I left?" Her voice trembles as she speaks, as if she doesn't really want to know the answer.

I take a sip of tea while collecting my thoughts. "Things settled down after about a week. People moved on to the next news story, you know? Your parents fought a lot. Not just at home, but in town as well. Then your dad disappeared. He didn't show up for work and no one saw him again. I don't know where he went."

Bayleigh sniffs, but nods for me to continue.

"Your mom stayed here, but we don't see her much. She's pretty reclusive."

Bayleigh nods slowly. "They were always so happy, you know? Such a great example of the perfect couple." She gives a weak smile. "We used to complain because they would kiss in front of us."

We both fall silent for a moment, and I'm lost in my memories. I can almost hear the echoes of our younger selves laughing and groaning as Bayleigh's parents stole kisses in the kitchen or embraced on the front porch swing. Those small displays of affection that once embarrassed us now seem precious and bittersweet.

"They really loved each other," I say softly. "And they adored you girls."

Bayleigh's eyes fill with tears. "We were so happy then. All of us. Sometimes I wake up and for a split second, I forget everything that's happened. I expect to hear Harper singing in the shower or smell Mom's cinnamon rolls baking." Her voice cracks. "But then reality comes crashing back."

I reach across the table and take her hand in mine. Her fingers are cold and trembling. "I'm so sorry, Bay."

She looks at my hand placed on top of hers for a moment before pulling away with a sharp movement. "What time is it? It must be late."

I look at my phone and see there are a bunch of texts and missed calls from Frankie and Kelly. "I think your assistant is worried about you. Do you want to call her?"

"I'll deal with her when I get back to the hotel."

I rise from my seat and leave some cash on the table to cover the cost of our meal.

Bayleigh watches me intently and says, "I'll make sure Kelly pays you back for this."

I shake my head, insisting that it's no trouble at all.

As we leave the restaurant, I offer to walk her back to the hotel. Without hesitation, she agrees, and we make the short journey in silence. Her bodyguard, so discreet, I forget he's even following us.

Once we reach the front of the hotel, I turn to her. "Thanks for tonight. That was fun."

"It was. Thank you for taking me and, well, everything."

She leans in and leaves a friendly kiss on my cheek, but I yearn for more.

I breathe her in for a moment before stepping away. "I'll see you tomorrow."

"Good night," she says, turns and starts walking into the hotel.

So many thoughts and feelings are running through my mind. She still has such an effect on me, even after all this time. Will it ever stop? Exhausted and with another full day of rehearsal ahead of me, I stay until she is out of sight before turning to leave.

At least after tonight, I have a bit more closure. Some of my questions have finally been answered, but I still have so many more. I wonder if I will ever get answers to them.

CHAPTER SEVENTEEN

ayleigh

MAX and I head up the elevator and to my room. He slips a key card from his pocket and enters before me to do a sweep of the suite. As I wait in the corridor, I let myself think of Harper.

Years of therapy have helped me understand that I tend to compartmentalize aspects of my life, especially when it comes to my childhood. I can't remember a time before Harper; she was born just three years after me.

We were more than sisters; we were best friends. We always knew we could count on each other for entertainment and support.

My passion for singing blossomed early on. I loved

listening to songs on the radio and memorizing all the lyrics. Harper would join me, and we'd started harmonizing together. Our bond grew stronger over the shared love of music.

It was Harper who came up with our first song lyrics. She shared the words with me one day, and I instantly heard a tune in my head. We never had a chance to finish that song though, as that fateful journey which would take her away from me occurred the very next day.

Max appears in the doorway and, with a nod, resumes his stance outside my door. I type a quick message to Kelly, letting her know that I am back safe and going to bed, and that I'll see her in the morning.

I head to the shower to wash the day off my skin. The warm water is comforting, and I start humming, lost in memories.

It's not until I wrap a towel around me that I recognize the notes replaying in my head and realize it's the song Harper and I started writing together. A song hidden away for so long, yet always bubbling close to the surface. I remember a line and sing it out loud, then frown. That's actually quite good.

I quickly put a dressing gown on then open the Notes app on my phone to record the lyrics.

It is as if I release a dam within me. The words pour out effortlessly, just as they did when Harper and I first wrote them together. Even though it has been eighteen years, the lyrics are still crystal clear in my mind.

I write and hum and sing, completely lost in the creative burst of inspiration. It's almost like Harper is sitting right beside me, and I am simply transcribing her thoughts. It's magical but also bittersweet.

As I reach the chorus, tears fall down my face. They start slowly at first, but soon turn into uncontrollable sobs. I set my phone down and curl up on my bed, overwhelmed by emotion.

"Harper, I'm so, so sorry." I weep as tears stream down my face and I finally let go of all the emotions I've been holding in for such a long time. The sorrow and regret consume me, a heavy weight on my soul. I weep for a life taken too soon, for the talent that will never be seen, and most of all, for my sister, who lost her life because of me. As exhaustion overtakes me, a single line from our song lingers on my lips:

"Our future was within reach, but fate had other plans, and now I'm left to pick up the shattered pieces of my soul."

* * *

I AM awoken the next morning by Kelly, who opens the curtains and lets light flood into the room. I rub my eyes and feel the stickiness of dried tears on my cheeks. I realize I fell asleep in my dressing gown, exhausted from the emotional release I had experienced the night before.

"You look like a mess," Kelly comments as she hands me a cup of takeaway coffee from the diner.

"Thanks," I say with a small smile, then taking a sip and immediately feel more awake. I search for my phone, afraid that last night's events were just a dream or that somehow the song has been deleted. Relieved, I find the notes still on my screen.

"Are you okay? You seem really stressed," Kelly asks, concern evident in her voice. I assure her that I am fine and simply had a late night. She sits down next to me on the bed, wearing a short black skirt and tight white shirt that accentuates her curvy figure.

"How did it go with Chase?" she asks eagerly.

Sitting cross-legged on the bed, I adjust my dressing gown so that only my bare legs are showing. "It went well. He did a good job."

Kelly looks at me expectantly for a moment, but when I don't offer any further details, she takes my coffee from my hand and sets it down on the bedside table. "I know how hard this week has been for you." She moves around the bed, comes up behind me, and puts her hands on my shoulders. "You're so tense." She applies just the right amount of pressure to my shoulders. It feels so good. She rubs, and I close my eyes and relax.

She pushes the dressing gown down so it slides over my shoulders and she touches my bare skin. Her hands are so soft and skillful. It's been a while since Kelly's touched me like this and I roll my stiff neck to release some tension.

"You know it's my job to look after you and keep

you happy." Her face is by my ear, her breath warming my skin. "I can help you relax. Would you like that?"

I know exactly what she means. Images of her riding Frankie yesterday flash through my mind, and moisture slicks across my pussy. I nod encouragingly, but keep my eyes closed as I think of how much I want to be touched, pleasured, and fucked.

Her hands glide over my breasts, pushing aside the loose dressing gown and exposing my bare body. I catch a glimpse of her in the mirror opposite and watch her with heavy-lidded eyes. She revels in this—serving me in any way I desire. I lay on my back across the bed, my legs dangling off the side. Then she positions my arms above my head before lowering her mouth to my breasts. "You can think of him if you want," she whispers before attending to my nipples.

Experience has taught me she knows exactly how to please me and has mastered the art of it. Her tongue swirls around my nipple before sucking firmly, sending me into a daze. She moves between my legs, and I lift my hips up for better access. Her fingers part my slick folds, and she rubs my clit gently. I moan loudly and she applies more pressure, causing me to writhe beneath her touch. Then she licks me from my entrance to my clit, igniting a fire within me. She repeats the motion, each time intensifying the pleasure. My arousal grows with each delicate suck on my nub while she pushes on my thighs, spreading me wider. The scent of my sex fills the air and I crave more, so much more. I grab onto my own breasts and massage them fervently as Kelly continues to suck harder.

She nuzzles her face between my legs, pressing against all of my sensitive flesh. I inhale sharply and grab onto her head, moving my hips in a frenzy against her mouth. She hums as she devours me, the vibrations intensifying my pleasure.

Then she adds her fingers into the mix, swirling them around inside of me before finding my G-spot and teasing it relentlessly.

"Fuck!" I beg for more, and she gives it to me faster and harder.

The thought of Chase watching us fills me with excitement, knowing how eager he would be to join in. We would position ourselves on the bed, offering up our asses for him to take. With one hand on each of our hips, he would thrust into us one at a time—her, then me, creating a perfect rhythm between all three of us. Our bodies would intertwine as we reached climax together, sharing our pleasure and juices.

As I come with a shudder and a long release, I can't help but think about these filthy scenarios that now occupy my mind. My heart races and my legs turn to jelly as I collapse onto the soft mattress.

"Do you feel better now?" Kelly asks, and I open my eyes to see her wipe some pussy juice from the side of her mouth and suck it off her finger.

I laugh on an exhale and nod. "Much better. Thank you."

She gives me that satisfied smirk of hers. "I'm always here to please."

Yes, she is. Did I mention Kelly is the best assistant ever? She has never asked me to fuck her, and after seeing her with Frankie, I know she enjoys sex just as much as I do. I've been with plenty of girls, and enjoyed myself immensely, but she has never wanted me to do anything to her. She's content with keeping me satisfied, and I'm not complaining.

It is just sex with her, though. There will never be anything more between us—unlike with Chase, who I have always felt amazing chemistry with. Chemistry that even now is undoubtedly still there. My thoughts turn to him, and I wonder if he is thinking of me this morning.

CHAPTER EIGHTEEN

hase

I'M NOT sure what Bayleigh did differently this morning, but her energy at rehearsal is much more lighthearted and carefree than it was the day before. She jokes with us, and we can't help but laugh along with her, making the time fly by. Her positive attitude seems to rub off on all of us, giving us a fresh burst of energy as well.

I couldn't sleep a wink last night, and to make matters worse, I climbed down the rabbit hole again and was up at two in the morning, watching every video I could find of Bayleigh. I watched music clips and interviews, and I even read tabloid articles about her. Amidst all the speculation about her personal life and the obstacles she has overcome, there is rarely any mention of her childhood.

Despite the challenges she has faced, they have shaped her into the strong woman she is today. She has fought her own battles with trauma and defeated alcoholism and drug addiction in order to be where she is now, fighting to keep her career and aspirations alive. I understand her struggles; she has always been a sensitive person, constantly under the public eye for most of her life. I often wonder how she has managed to keep Harper out of the media's attention all this time—it would make for a juicy story. However, I am grateful for both our sakes that her death has been kept under wraps. I received enough sympathetic looks years ago when it first happened. Now, it is just a distant memory that most people have forgotten about.

But not everyone has forgotten. Even with therapy, I can still vividly remember every detail of that fateful night. No amount of counseling will ever erase it from my mind. God knows I've tried.

Kelly orders us lunch and we sit around on chairs, eating sandwiches and fries. The members of the band are more relaxed today too, no longer on edge.

This band is new, and I learn that many members have come and gone over the years. Bayleigh has adapted to being able to play with anyone as only a truly experienced and confident performer can. She doesn't have to rely on her musicians to support her. But having heard them all play together today, I know that having a team here, supporting and backing her, makes a huge difference. And that's really what Bayleigh needs in her life. She puts on a strong façade, but behind it she's still just a lonely teenage girl, wanting people to like her.

These musicians are cool, honest people. Perhaps they will stick around and help her after this gig. A part of me wants to stick around too. I want to be there, holding her hand and protecting her from the haters of the world.

But even if I could get past all the hurt and pain that she's put me through, I can't be sure she'd even want me. We're on different paths and have different needs. A fish and a bird could never coexist.

I think of some of the rumors about her shows. The many performances where she'd shown up drunk or high and the band had had to do their best to cover for her. The last show she performed was the worst, though. Security had to pull her off stage before she hurt herself. The way she was slandered in the news and online after that was painful to read. Her reputation seemed all but shattered.

But it seems that her stint in rehab really has changed her now. What did they say about addicts? They have to hit rock bottom before they can truly find their way out.

By midafternoon we've rehearsed the full set, and Bayleigh calls it a day. The others slink off, by I'm still buzzing with excitement, not wanting this feeling to end.

"Does Kelly have a full evening planned for you?" I ask as I join her at the table where my guitar case sits open.

She looks up at me. "Fortunately, she gave me a night off. I stayed up late last night, so I'm looking forward to a quiet night."

I take a swig from my water bottle. "What kept you up?"

She looks at me, her eyes narrowing as though she's contemplating what to tell me.

"Actually, after I got back to my room, I started playing with some lyrics."

"You did?" My eyes widen in disbelief. "But you said you didn't write anymore."

She gives me a shrug and a playful smile. "I felt inspired after our talk, and the words just kind of flowed out of me." There is a glint in her eye that I recognize. She used to have it but this is the first time since she's been back that I've seen it. It's pure passion and inspiration.

"That's great," I say. "Can you show me?"

She bites her lip before speaking again. "Actually, would you mind helping me with the backing melody?"

"I'd love to." The grin she gives me is priceless. We drag over two chairs to the wooden table, and I strum my guitar while she pulls out her cell phone and shows me the lyrics she's written. I read them through a few times, taking in the mix of joy and sorrow, and I it sounds to me like she is drawing inspiration from Harper. This must be her way of coping. The words are filled with raw emotion, blending together in a beautiful form of poetry.

My fingers dance across the strings, warming up with a few chords before starting to improvise. The first three notes are quick and then some slow ones follow. The combination repeats as I begin to hum her lyrics. Bayleigh nods along to the beat, joining in on the singing. The first line sends shivers down my spine.

She closes her eyes as she lets the words flow out, releasing the emotions she's been holding onto. I sing the next verse alongside her, our voices melding together in perfect harmony. As she sings with such passion and intensity, it sends tingles throughout my entire body. This is pure magic. Nothing but pure magic fills the air as we sing together for the first time in years. It takes every ounce of self-control not to pause and make love to her right here in this room. The way her body moves with the music ignites something inside of me like never before. And her voice? Absolute perfection. The other songs on her playlist may not be hers, but this song is different—it's full of emotion and feelings straight from her soul. I can see for myself why she's such a star. She has that special something, and I am honored to be a part of it.

I continue with the chorus, but when it's time for her solo, I step back and let her shine. My heart beats faster as she belts out the lyrics, her eyes never leaving mine. I watch her intently as she sings the chorus, loving the combination of her voice and my guitar. When her voice deepens and she truly gets lost in the emotions of the words, it hits me—she was meant to do this.

I sing the final chorus with her. As our voices fade into silence, we both sit there, staring at each other. I can hear her breathing quicken and see the movement of her slender neck as she swallows. I am completely mesmerized by her. She is like the pied piper, and I am a foolish teenager again, following her around like a lovesick puppy. Does she even realize the hold she has over me?

Suddenly, she breaks eye contact and stands up. We are so close that her knee brushes against mine, and I instinctively raise my hand to rest on her thigh. I don't want this moment to end. She parts her soft lips slightly, and it's enough of an invitation for me. I can't resist any longer. I stand and look down at her, taking in the shine of her golden hair. I reach out a hand to play with one curly strand that falls around her face.

Being this close, I can see the tiny freckles sprinkled across her nose, reminding me of when we used to count them together during lazy summer days on the ranch.

"Chase." My name escapes her lips in a breathy whisper, and she leaves her mouth slightly open. She looks so inviting, and I can't resist the urge to see if she still tastes like strawberries and sunshine.

When she doesn't pull away, I run my fingers across the nape of her neck. Her pulse is thumping out of control. Mine feels the same way. I slowly lean in. "Is this okay with you?"

Her eyelids flutter closed, and she nods ever so slightly.

Our mouths brush against each other as I hold her in place. Her lips part slightly, inviting me in. I have to hold my breath and make myself not take more than she's willing to give me right now.

I want this moment to last, to savor every touch and sensation. It takes all of my self-control to pull back and rest my forehead against hers.

"Bay?" I ask. Her name sounds like music on my lips. I've avoided using it for so long that now it feels like a treat when I say it out loud. She moans softly, her eyes still closed, and I can't help myself any longer. Leaning in again, I kiss her, deeper the kiss, tangling my tongue with hers and pulling her closer to me.

When I finally break away, everything that I'm feeling is reflected back at me on her face. Using my thumb, I gently wipe her bottom lip, needing one last touch before moving away from her.

But as I start to pull back completely, she grabs onto my shirt tightly. Turning my head to look at her, I see that her eyes are filled with pure lust and desire. It makes me ache with need.

"I need you, Chase," she pleads. "Come up to my room with me."

Despite knowing that I should refuse, I find myself unable to resist. In this empty room, all I can think about is taking her. Every inch of her ivory skin, every taste of her lush pussy—I want it all. I want to be with her as a man, not just some hormone-driven teenager. I need to prove to myself that our connection is purely chemical and not some destined soul mate bullshit. But deep down, I know there's something inexplicable drawing us together. My logical mind warns me that this will only end in heartbreak, but my body craves her like oxygen. I want to feel alive again, and the only way I know how is with her by my side. She's the only one who can make me feel truly alive.

CHAPTER NINETEEN

ayleigh

I FEEL it in his body the moment he gives in and stops fighting this craving and need we have for each other. To hell with the future—I only know I need him now.

I take his hand in mine before he can change his mind and lead him to the elevator. Max is following behind us, and I don't care what he thinks of me taking Chase to my suite. I don't pay him for his opinions—only his protection and discretion.

He opens the door ahead of us, and we pause as Max sweeps the room before allowing us in. I close the door softly behind him and take a calming breath to steady my pounding heart before turning to see Chase.

He watches me with darkened eyes as I take my

time approaching him. I have lived off the memories of him for eighteen years, and now that he's ready and willing in front of me, I am nervous. My body has changed. I'm not the innocent young girl I once was. What if he sees my scars and they repulse him? What if I don't live up to the memory?

His lips part and I swallow. "Come here." He stretches out his arms to me, and I walk as though being pulled toward him by a magnet.

His strong arms encircle me, pulling me closer as he passionately kisses my lips. I hold on to his T-shirt tightly, wanting to be even closer to him. He changes the angle of our kiss, urging me for more. The hardness of his desire presses against my stomach, and I instinctively press my body against his, moving in sync with him. He breaks away from my mouth and begins kissing down my cheekbone and neck, causing shivers to run down my spine. As I tilt my head back for him, he continues to nibble and suck on my earlobe, making my body tingle with anticipation. Normally a dominant partner in the bedroom, I willingly surrender to his touch and kisses without hesitation. His hands move to undo the buttons on my top, exposing me fully to him.

He gasps and my eyelids burst open, searching for the reason why he's stopped. I look down and see him fingering my necklace. *His* necklace.

"You're wearing it." His voice is barely a whisper as

he rubs his thumb over the smooth wooden carving. "I saw the chain the other day, but didn't realise."

"I never take it off." My voice breaks as emotions threaten to consume me.

He turns his attention from the bird carefully carved from wood around my neck to my eyes. "You don't?"

I nod. "It's the most precious thing I own," I say. "Because you made it for me."

He searches my eyes for a moment, then presses his lips first to the carving, then to my lips. His breath on my skin is a warm, steamy rush of air.

My legs turn to jelly as I am overcome with desire. I lean against his strong body for support, feeling the heat of his thighs against mine, the roughness of his stubble on my skin, and the firmness in his grip as he holds onto my hips. My craving for more intensifies, and our breaths become one as our tongues dance in perfect harmony. We move towards the bed together, never breaking our passionate kiss. He slowly lowers me onto the soft sheets and hovers above me.

His fingers trace down my face and neck, and into the curves of my cleavage before he pulls down the straps of my bra and caresses my breasts with his palm. I arch my back in pleasure, wanting more of his touch. With one swift motion, he releases the other strap and takes my taut nipple into his mouth. A surge of electricity shoots through me and settles as a low, tingling sensation in my core. I wrap my legs around him, pulling him closer to where I crave his pressure the most. The sound of his amused chuckle fills the room, but in this moment, I don't care how greedy I may seem. His slow exploration of my body is almost too much to handle. When he moves and takes my other nipple into his mouth, the same electrifying effect ripples through me and I grind against him, trying to create the friction that I desperately need.

"You're so fucking hot right now, and I want to cherish this moment." He says, and I drop my head back in pleasure and frustration.

My heart races with excitement, my body craving his touch. He moves his hand behind me to unclasp my bra, and there is a rush of warmth as it falls away from my skin. He presses himself against me and our passionate kiss intensifies, overwhelming me with desire. His skin against mine is like magic, and I want to feel every inch of him. I yearn for his heat, his heartbeat, and the intense emotions he elicits in me. As he breaks our kiss and trails his lips down my neck, chest, and belly, I whimper in anticipation. He expertly removes my jeans, placing kisses along my legs as he goes. His fingers trace back up my legs and grip onto my hips before slipping beneath the waistband of my underwear. His touch is light but sends shivers through me as he teases my folds. He groans in pleasure, and I love how desperate he sounds—it only fuels my own desire. With hooded eyes, I watch as he removes his finger and puts it into his mouth, tasting me on his skin. Kelly was amazing this morning, but it's different with Chase. There's history between us and feelings I can't even begin to describe. No one else makes me feel the way he does.

"Fuck." I bite my lip and lift up my ass up, and he slides my soaked panties down my hips and over my legs.

Once they're pulled from my toes, he pauses and takes me in. He stares at me, his intense gaze giving me the confidence to lie here naked, completely exposed to him. He sees me for me—not the performer, and not my alter ego. Just me. Bay. *His* Bay.

His eyes are dark and his mouth slightly open. I watch as he breathes deeply, his chest rising and falling.

For a brief, intense moment, our eyes meet before he leans down towards me. I shift my weight back onto my arms and the anticipation builds as his head draws lower. His warm breath on my skin sends shivers along my spine as he continues down to my aching pussy.

The first touch of his tongue on my clit nearly pushes me over the edge. I jerk involuntarily, but Chase's hands grip onto my thighs, keeping me still. He presses closer, his tongue moving quickly and hungrily against me as he kisses me with urgency. With every flick, nibble, and suck from his skilled tongue, my muscles burn with pleasure.

His hands slide up to my hips as he pulls me even closer to him, fully enveloping himself between my legs. I grind against him eagerly, loving the friction of his stubble against my sensitive skin. My back arches and my thighs tremble as an intense orgasm washes over me unexpectedly. Chase continues to pleasure me, drinking in my juices with hunger still evident in his actions.

I gasp for air, trembling with an arousal that is almost too much to handle. But Chase is relentless. I grab a handful of his hair and use it to guide his head back up towards mine. His gaze is hazy and unfocused as he looks up at me, a wet sheen covering his face. Tenderly, I wipe it away with gentle strokes of my hand across his mouth.

"Fuck, you taste so good," he murmurs as he moves slowly up the bed.

I slide my hands down his chest, then pull his shirt up and over his head. He shifts onto his back, and I prop myself up to admire him. His body is toned and muscular, and I trace my fingers over every bump and crevice. Lowering my head, I kiss his warm skin while a strand of my hair falls in front of my face. He brushes it away and watches me. I find one of his nipples and take it between my lips, eliciting a deep exhale from him. My tongue and fingers make their way across his chest and stomach, exploring every inch with care.

His hand meets mine at the front of his jeans, and I pause to watch as he slowly unbuttons them one by one. His erection lies concealed behind the black fabric of his boxer briefs, and I sit up to help him remove the rest of his clothing until his erection juts large and proud in front of me, and I sigh. *Hello, old friend.*

He raises his arm and rests it on the back of his head, a gesture that always makes me smile. I can't resist wrapping my hand around his cock and licking my lips at the sight of pre-cum coating the tip. A moan escapes his lips, urging me to lean in and lick it off. His eyes close briefly before he opens them again, placing his hands encouragingly on the back of my neck.

I position myself and slowly take his swollen head into my mouth. My tongue swirls around it, feeling him grow harder beneath me. I move up and down his thick length with long strokes, fighting the urge to gag as he hits the back of my throat. His hand entwines in my hair, urging me to quicken my pace until I can feel his muscles tighten on the edge of climax. As much as I crave his release in my mouth, right now I want to feel him inside me more. I pull away with a wet sound and reach for the bedside table where Kelly always leaves condoms for such occasions. She knows to do this in every hotel room, just in case. And more often than not, I end up needing them.

I tear open the packet with my teeth and offer it to him. He takes it and covers himself with one hand. Once he's ready, I straddle him and slowly sink down onto him, empaling myself on his cock. The mix of emotions and the way his body fits with mine over-whelms me, causing me to arch my back and let out a loud moan as he fills me completely. My hips move in circular motions, and I'm savoring every sensation.

Our lips meet, and he kisses me with a ferocity that shows his need for me. As I rock on top of him, he loses control. With my eyes closed and my hands gripping the headboard, I set a rhythm that neither of us can maintain for long. Every movement and touch from him elicits a deep moan from my lips.

I welcome his cock as he strokes inside me, feeling every inch of him stretching and filling me. Each thrust sends shivers down my spine and builds desire in the pit of my stomach once again. Our eyes meet as we connect in this intimate moment, and I'm both completely focused and lost in pleasure.

"You feel so good, Bay. So fucking good," he murmurs as his hands tighten their grip on my hips.

"So do you, Chase. You feel perfect."

My hips move in sync with his, thrusting harder. I tilt my hips to increase the intensity of his penetration. I can sense when he reaches his limit, his neck arching back and our bodies slamming together in one final, deep stroke. He exhales loudly, almost as if he's sobbing. I forget to breathe as the last shudders of his body push me over the edge into my own climactic release. My muscles tighten around him, drawing out the last of his orgasm while I am lost in the sensation of him inside and all around me. My heart is still racing in my chest as I slide off Chase's hips and collapse beside him, immersed in a heavenly pool of blissful sensations.

After disposing of the used condom, he pulls me close to him and I nestle my head against his arm. Both of us are breathing heavily, but otherwise we are silent. I long to see his face, to know what he's thinking. In my years in Nashville, I've had many lovers. Men and women have thrown themselves at me, all eager to say they've slept with Bayleigh Gilmore. But it's never felt like this with anyone else. Not even with Chase when we were teenagers, exploring our own bodies and each other's. This is something more than I'd ever expected.

"That was . . ." His voice trails off on a sigh, and I grin.

"Amazing." I push up onto my shoulder so I can look at him. I'm not going to regret this for one moment. "You're amazing."

As his eyes cloud over and his lips part, I know what's coming. But I don't want to hear him say he regrets it or that it can never be repeated.

I know that if I keep his mouth busy, he won't be able to break my heart.

CHAPTER TWENTY

hase

BAYLEIGH RUNS her fingers through my hair and kisses me, causing any argument I may have had to dissipate in a rush of lust and desire. I stroke her cheek with my hand, and I move it through her soft curls. Those damn curls always get to me. "I fucking love your hair," I whisper as her lips trace along my jawline.

My intense desire for her makes me hard again within seconds as she presses herself against me. My hand trails from her hair to one of her perfect breasts, playing with the perky peak and causing her to moan into my neck.

It's not like me to go for another round so soon, but tonight my body defies me. It must be because I've never felt this kind of fiery attraction with anyone else before. As her lips nibble on my earlobe, my cock springs back to life and the urgency to have her grows stronger.

I can't get enough of her. I never will. But I push that thought away and decide to take whatever she offers for as long as possible. My hand moves down to her stomach, and she opens her legs, allowing me access. She's still wet from her last orgasm and my fingers slide easily inside her, exploring and pleasuring every inch of her. I roll her onto her back and watch as she closes her eyes and arches her back against the bed while I continue to pleasure her hot, delicious pussy.

"Yes," she cries out as I rub her clit. "Yes, that's so good."

I could come again just watching her beautiful face as she gives in to her pleasure. She moves her hips like she's dancing and yearning for more.

"I want you in me, Chase." The way she says my name, practically singing it, is the sweetest sound I've ever heard.

"You want me, Bayleigh?" I ask her. "You want me to fuck you again?"

"Oh God, yes!"

I reach past her and find a fresh condom, then put it on as quickly as I can. I don't know how long I can last this time; I already feel full and close to coming again.

She pulls me closer as I position myself above her,

ready to enter. She meets my body eagerly and I push into her with force.

"Hard and fast," she pleads, locking her eyes with mine. "Please."

I nod in agreement and give her what she asks for. Each time I penetrate deeper, and with every withdrawal, I long for her. I let her take complete control of my body, using it like an instrument to bring us both to the edge of ecstasy.

My arms hold on to her tightly as we move together rhythmically. "I can feel you, Bayleigh," I say as her body tightens around me, signaling she's close to coming. "You feel amazing."

She cries out loudly and clings onto my hips as I drive into her one final time before losing control and releasing inside her. "Holy shit."

I bury my face in the crook of her neck and inhale her intoxicating scent—a mix of flowers, sex, and Bayleigh. I can never get enough of it.

We both lie on our sides afterwards, cuddled close to each other. "Let's stay like this tonight," she whispers.

We both know we should probably talk about what's just happened, but in that moment, all I want is to hold on to Bayleigh Gilmore and bask in the afterglow of our passion.

"Go to sleep, love," I say against her hair. "I'm not going anywhere."

CHAPTER TWENTY-ONE

ayleigh

KELLY'S MORNING knock sounds a moment before the blonde assistant enters the suite with her usual chirpy: "Good morning."

Suddenly wide awake, Chase quickly pulls a sheet up to cover our naked bodies and I let out a chuckle. It's not like she hasn't seen me in bed with someone before. But I don't tell Chase this. He already knows about many of my flaws. I don't need to add *sex addict* to the list.

Kelly puts one of her hands on her hip and holds a coffee cup in the other and grins down at us. "Hi."

"Kelly." Chase nods in her direction.

She turns to me, her eyebrows raised high. "Bayleigh, your coffee." She puts it on the bedside table closest to me. "I'll give you guys a minute." Then leaves the room.

I look at Chase, and he smirks at me. "I guess that's my cue." He kisses me quickly then rolls out of bed. I gaze at his perfect ass as he picks up his clothes.

"You know, you don't have to go if you don't want." I like the idea of us being able to have a quickie whenever the mood takes us.

"That's tempting, Bay." He kisses me quickly on the lips before straightening and zipping up his pants. "But I have to get back to the ranch and get some work done before we rehearse later."

"Okay. I'll see you later then."

He grabs the rest of his belongings and waves back at me. "See you later."

As the door snicks closed, Kelly comes into the bedroom and sits next to me. "Spill."

I lie back against the pillow and drape an arm over my eye. "We stayed up working on my song and one thing led to another."

"And how was the sex?"

I look up at her and see her run her tongue over her top lip. "It was . . . I mean, it's different with him."

"Shit, was it bad?"

"Fuck no. It was the total opposite of bad. It was the best!"

"Hey!" She pushes me playfully, and I smile back at her.

"Present company excluded, of course. He was the best sex I've had with a man."

"Thank you." She mock bows. "Are you guys going to hook up again? I mean, so I know what to expect in the mornings."

I shrug. "I dunno. I mean, we leave in three days."

"Exactly! You got to get it while you can." Kelly jiggles her shoulders.

"I don't want to think about that. I just want to enjoy this moment right now."

"Great. Well, on that note, you need to call Brendon back at some point today," she says and stands up from the bed, carefully brushing down her silk pants.

"What does he want?" It could be to deliver yet more bad news. That would definitely kill my vibe. I reach over and sip my coffee. It's lukewarm, so I drain it quickly. "I'm going to need more coffee before that conversation."

Kelly looks at her watch. "I can send Max for another. I really need to finalize the backstage passes for the show on Saturday. They're due in this afternoon, and we have a lot of label reps coming for it."

"No bother," I climb out of bed, "I feel like a walk." I slip into the bathroom and turn on the shower. I can feel Chase's cum, warm and sticky, dribbling down my thighs. I clench my legs together as I relive the experience of his hands on my waist, his big, thick cock pounding into me. Fuck, I could come again, just thinking about him.

I get under the steaming water and let it caress my sensitive skin, lost in memories of what we did to each other and all the things I still want to do with him. To him.

I wonder if he leaves all his sexual partners like this —eager for more. Or if it's just me.

I rarely have the same partner more than once, unless, like Kelly, they are very talented with their tongue. But I can see myself having Chase over and over again. I love how he makes my body feel. How he knew what to do. How he played me like he played his guitar. Building me up, up and strumming my body until I climaxed. And what a climax it was—like I released eighteen years' worth of desire and need.

I finish in the shower and wrap a plush towel around my body before opening the door. Kelly is waiting for me, dangling hangers of clothes from her finger. "Anything else I can help you with?" She raises an eyebrow.

"Not right now." I take the clothes from her. "Thanks."

I dress in a jeans-and-T-shirt combo and dry my hair, scrunching it the way I was taught and adding gel to the ringlets. After applying some makeup, I leave the bathroom.

Kelly is busy at the desk, working on her laptop. "Where are my scarves?" I ask.

She turns and rises from her chair. "Which one do you want?"

"The grey with the butterflies," I say as she moves to a dresser and opens a drawer.

"Good choice." She hands me the scarf and watches me as I stand in front of the full-length mirror and tie it. Once I'm happy with my appearance, Kelly hands me my bag. "Have fun, and don't forget to call Brendon."

"Yes, boss," I reply as I open the door and see Max waiting for me. "Let's go." I smile at him.

We head down the lift and through the lobby where we run into Mr. Dobson, who stops to ask me again how our stay is. I give him a smile and thank him. "Everything is great."

"We are so excited about the show and the weather forecast is another cloud-free night."

Clear weather is perfect for an outdoor show, but I'm sure the town would trade it in for some decent rainfall.

Once outside, I turn my eyes up to the clear blue sky. The air is dry and warm. No respite in sight for the town.

I wander down the street and forget about my shadow. I'm just a girl walking through town on her way to get coffee. The people here are used to me now —it's not like I'm getting mobbed as I go for a stroll. I forgot how this felt—living like a normal person.

When I come to the diner, I open the door and have

to stand in line behind a few people waiting to order. I'm feeling so chill it doesn't even bother me. I gaze at the menu on the wall. When did coffee get so complicated?

When I get to the front of the line, I give my order to the young woman.

"Is that to have here or takeaway?" she asks.

I look around and find a couple of empty seats, but then change my mind and decide instead to go for a walk. "Takeaway please." I find the card in the bag, pay, and stand aside to wait.

My gaze meets a lady's, who is sitting with her two children having breakfast. She's about my age and their table is filled with pancakes and grits. I smile at her. That could have been me if I'd stayed here. Raising kids of my own.

She rises from her chair and walks over to me. "Excuse me, Ms. Gilmore, but could I get a picture with you?"

"Of course," I agree and wait for her to prepare her phone and get into position. I smile back at the image of us on her screen as she takes the selfie. Yep, I could have been her if my life had taken a different course.

"Thank you." She lowers the phone and turns to me. "We're in town because we won tickets to come to your show. We're so excited"

I touch her arm. Fans love it when I do that, and this lady is no exception, gazing at my hand like I have the Midas touch. "Where do you live?"

"On a farm about forty miles from here. We're one of them hit bad by the drought, so you being here and helping raise money means so much to us." Her eyes glisten, and I lean in and give her a hug.

"I'm prayin' for y'all," I say, and she smiles back at me.

"Thank you so much."

"Are these your kids?" I ask, gesturing at the boy and girl who are watching us. They look skinny. This may be the biggest meal they've had in a while.

"Yes, would you mind saying hello?"

"Please." I follow her to the table, and she introduces me to the freckled, brown-haired children that look so much like her. "Pete and June, say hello to Ms. Gilmore."

They smile at me like I'm just some friend of their mom's, not a famous singer, and it makes me smile. I'm not famous to everybody, and that is fine.

"Hi kids. Are y'all having a nice visit in Sweetgum Valley?"

They nod and continue eating hungrily. Their mother turns to me and speaks quietly. "We don't come to town often. I apologize for their manners."

"No apologies necessary," I say as my order is called out. I turn to acknowledge the waitress, then turn back to the lady. "What's your name?"

"Lorraine," she replies.

"You have a great visit, Lorraine, and thank you for coming to my show."

I turn and go to the counter, where I wave at the waitress to come over. When she does, I hand over the credit card again. "Can you please charge Lorraine's bill to this?" I glance back to their table and notice they don't have any drinks. "And whatever drinks they want, too. I think those kids would like some chocolate milkshakes, but check with their mom first."

The waitress processes the card before handing it back to me. I collect my coffee and wave to Lorraine as I leave the diner.

Outside, I pull out my phone and dial Brendon, who picks up quickly.

"Bayleigh, how's it going in 'the valley'?"

I roll my eyes. "That's not what we call it here."

He chuckles. "Maybe you could start calling it that. Could get it trending! Anyway, that's not why I wanted to speak to you.

I continue wandering around town aimlessly, Max following silently behind me, while Brendon catches me up on business. "All your publicity is really paying off and making your image more wholesome. I got to say I'm really glad you're following my advice on this."

So far this trip hasn't been as bad as I thought. Especially last night. Totally worth it.

"How are rehearsals going? The new guy picking it up?"

"Yeah, he's really good. He fits in with the band well and has picked up the songs super-fast. It's quite impressive, actually."

"That's great." There's excitement in his voice as he continues, "They want to live-stream the event so we can't have any mistakes in this."

My eyes widen, and I stop walking. "Live-stream? Really?"

"That's right, kid; the reach could be insane. Mathew is pulling in the younger audience and you've got the hometown advantage. He's even been doing the media rounds to promote it. You didn't see his *Tonight Show* appearance yesterday? It was epic."

Once upon a time that would have been me, doing all the TV shows and radio appearances. Now all the best promo spots are going to the young cowboy. I try not to let the news hurt my ego, but it definitely still stings.

"What can I do?" I don't want to be seen as riding Mathew's coattails. "I have time to kill here."

"Well, you could go to that bar again. Get seen helping out the town—you know the drill."

"Okay. Have you been sent any more songs for me?" I ask, eager to start making more music again.

"Nothing great. We need something authentic and meaningful for this one."

My first albums were sexy and controversial, then as I grew older they became raw and gritty with a lot of pent-up anger. I don't want to go back to either of those styles. I want to make music that can inspire and heal. Music might have been the cause of my pain, but it can also be a kind of therapy. If I want this album to be a true representative of me, I need more creative input. I need to write.

"I've actually been doing some writing. The new guitar player has been helping me put my lyrics to music."

"No kidding! Maybe we should hire him full time!" Brendon laughs. "Can you send me a demo?"

Anxiety rises in my throat. What if he doesn't like it? What if I'm not good enough or talented enough of a writer, and everyone hates it and laughs at me? Then what?

"Are you sure? It's the first song I've written in forever. It could be terrible."

"How will I know that if you don't let me hear it? Send it through, and I'll tell you if it's something we can work with. Now, I gotta go. Keep practicing." He hangs up, and I'm left with the phone still at my ear, the line gone.

I look at my cell and open the Notes app and reread the song again, singing it in my head. It really is good. Chase likes it and he knows music. Maybe this is how I move forward and recreate myself. I write my own music my way. The idea has me smiling like a goofball. I love this idea so much. I fall into a daydream as I wander the footpaths. Lyrics and tunes pour in as though they had been building up behind a dam and now are flooding out. I start typing them as I walk, scared to lose my flow.

Minutes later, I finally look up and stop. Where

even am I? I turn around and stop abruptly. What the actual fuck?

In front of me stands a dilapidated house, its once bright paint now peeling, and the shutters broken. Weeds and overgrown grass have taken over the yard, giving it an abandoned appearance.

But this is not how it has always been. It used to be a warm and loving home, where my family of four lived and grew up. Where we spent holidays and birthdays together. Now, as I stand in front of it, I can't help but feel a sense of longing for those happy memories.

I put away my phone and look back at Max. "Stay here. I'll just be a minute." Max opens his mouth, but I hold up my hand. "Wait here." Then I step through the weeds towards the front door. Looking through the dirty windows, I can see that the familiar furniture inside is still arranged, just as I remember. The house is dark and empty, giving off an eerie feeling.

Despite knowing that I should just leave this ghostly house and return to my hotel, I can't resist the urge to go inside. I want to see if I still belong here—if I can somehow feel Harper's presence inside. So, I turn the doorknob and enter the unlocked and seemingly unloved house.

As I walked through the halls, memories flood back to me. My father's faded recliner sits in the same spot, no doubt untouched since he moved out. The old television and couch are still set up in the living room where Harper and I would watch music videos and cartoons together. A small smile spreads across my face as I remember all the fun times we shared.

But it is upstairs where I truly want to be. As I make my way up the creaky staircase, my eyes are drawn to the framed photos lining the wall. Happy moments frozen in time, each one featuring Harper's radiant smile. My throat tightens as I look at the last photo, taken just a few months before the accident. It is a picture of us hugging at the lake on a warm summer day—a memory that I haven't thought about in years, but one that I will never forget.

At the top of the stairs, I push open the door to my old room. It is like stepping back in time. My dresser, lamp, and posters are all exactly as I had left them. The musty air reminds me that this room hasn't been aired out in a long time—it's almost like a mausoleum for my past.

But as I look around. I no longer felt connected to the girl who used to live here. I have grown up and moved on, while she's remained stuck in this room. A sudden noise makes me jump and knock into my dresser, causing an ornament to fall to the ground.

My mother stands in the doorway, looking much older than she actually is with greying hair and shabby clothes. Her voice is harsh as she asks, "What are you doing here?"

It is then that I realize just how much this house has changed and how far away from it all I have drifted.

"The door was unlocked." I say with a shaky voice.

She may be small, but she looks frightening and not at all as I remember her.

"I live here," she says, "and I didn't invite you in."

"I just . . ." I gesture around the room. "It's exactly the same."

"I never had a reason to change it, so why should I?"

I'm not sure what to say. This woman is a stranger to me. All the love and warmth is gone, and it seems that just a shell is left. I should go; I need to get out of here.

I move toward the door, but when she doesn't move to let me pass, I stop in front of her.

"Why are you here, Bayleigh?" She shoots me an accusatory look, and a lump forms in my throat.

"I'm sorry. I shouldn't have come."

"No, you shouldn't have." Her voice drips with animosity. "You shouldn't have come back to this town, either. You're not wanted here."

I swallow hard as my eyes burn. "I'm sorry—I've said it a thousand times."

"And it will never be enough. It will never bring your sister back. You ruined everything." She narrows her dark eyes at me, and it's like she's shooting daggers into my heart.

"You are a disappointment. Look at what you've done with your life! Drugs, alcohol! Harper would never have turned out like this. She was a beautiful girl, inside and out. You're worthless."

My stomach twists painfully, and I feel like I might

vomit. Her words cut me deeply as she spews out all of the insecurities that I've always believed about myself. I shrink back, feeling small and insignificant. I am the reason my sister is no longer alive and not living the beautiful life she was meant for. I don't deserve to be happy.

"You should be punished for what you did."

I lose my balance and collapse to my knees, unable to hold back the sobs that wrack me. "It was an accident." My voice cracks pitifully. "I'm sorry. I'm so sorry."

But my mother shows no empathy—only hatred. "I wish you would just disappear and never come back."

I raise my eyes to her and wipe my tear-stained face with the back of my hands. "How can you say that to your own daughter?"

"You are not my daughter anymore. You are dead to me."

Nothing can hurt me more than her cruel words. We will never be close again; she will never forgive me or show me any love.

"Now . . ." She steps back and gestures to the door for me to leave. "Get out of my house and never come back."

With shaky legs, I push myself up from the ground. I sniffle and gather the last bit of strength within me. "Goodbye, Mother." And then I run as fast as I can, down the stairs and out the door. I collide with Max's solid chest as I rush off the porch.

"Are you okay, ma'am?" he asks, looking me over for injuries.

"Yes, let's just get away from here." I pull out of from his embrace and start speed-walking away. I continue to walk, leaving that house and all its painful memories behind me.

CHAPTER TWENTY-TWO

ayleigh

As I turn onto Main Street, I put on my big, dark sunglasses and straighten myself up as best as possible. Not that this day could get any worse. My phone rings, and I pick it up to see Kelly's picture on the screen. I put it back in my bag. I don't want to talk to anyone. My mother was right; I am a waste of a life. I spy a liquor store, and there is only a moment of doubt in my mind before I open the door and head inside. I keep my eyes low as I pay for the whiskey and head back outside.

Max stands in front of me, blocking my path. "That's not a good idea."

I look up at his intimidating face. "It's got nothing to do with you." I try to sidestep him, but he blocks me again. "Get the fuck out of my way!"

"You hired me to protect you," he reminds me, "and right now, the only person you need protecting from is yourself."

"In that case, you're fired! Now get the fuck away from me!" From the corner of my eye, I see a couple look at us as they walk past. But nothing can stop me now. Who the hell cares about a career? I'm nothing. All I want is to numb this burning pain of unworthiness. I want to fall asleep and never wake up again. I want an end to all this pain.

I push into Max's shoulder and he lets me pass, but follows closely behind. As I walk, I unscrew the lid and raise the bottle to my lips.

Fuck everything. I allow the strong amber liquid to fill my mouth, then I gulp it down.

I wait for that feeling of oblivion to take over, and when it doesn't come, I take another gulp. And then another.

My steps become a bit wobbly, and my mind has a nice dull feel to it. I look at the bottle, which is much lighter now.

I spy a grassy park and head over to it, then collapse on a park bench. I close my eyes to stop the spinning of my vision. I can hear the birds singing and the noise of children laughing in the distance. I gulp down the rising bile bubbling in my stomach. I don't want to think about all the terrible things I have down. All the people I have hurt.

Like Chase. He deserves so much more than me. I'm no good for anyone. I'm a disease. A terrible, terrible person.

Chase is so good. He's smart and kind and beautiful. He should get married and have lots of babies. Pretty blond babies.

I lose track of time as I cover my face against the sun.

My eyes burn again, but I refuse to shed any more tears. I reach for my bottle next to me, but it's gone. "Who took my…?"

I open my eyes and a dark shadow looms in front of me.

"Chase?" Am I imagining it's him? Surely that's all this is. Just my stupid imagination.

"Bay, what have you done?" It is his voice. I blink and squint until his face comes into view.

He sits on the bench next to me and puts his arm around me. He feels so good and smells delicious.

I snuggle in close. I feel so safe and secure in his embrace. "Can we just stay like this forever?"

His fingers brush up and down my arm tenderly. "What happened?'

I squeeze my eyes together as a memory of my mother fills my vision. I shake my head. "I don't want to talk about it."

"Okay," he says, and his lips press against my forehead. I want more of his touch. So much more. I want to feel anything other than what I'm feeling now.

I want to feel . . . wanted.

I move until I find his lips and kiss him. He kisses me briefly, but then pulls back. "You've been drinking."

I search out his mouth again, but this time he holds me away from him. "Why? Why would you do this?"

It all comes back to me then with sobering sharpness, and I feel like my heart is being sliced apart.

"My parents kicked me out because I killed Harper. They hate me. They blame me." Anger rises through me. "It's all my fault, isn't it? I can't do anything right!" I stand and the world starts to spin, but when Chase tries to help me, I push him away.

"Let me help." The concern on his face reminds me of why I don't let anyone too close.

"I don't need your help. I don't need anything from you." I turn my back to him and take a steadying breath. I can't drag Chase into this. No one should have to suffer with me. I can't hurt anyone else. Especially not Chase. I've already hurt him too much. "We can't do this, Chase."

"Do what? Tell me, what is wrong?"

"This! You and me. Nothing can come of us. We live in totally different worlds, and I don't deserve you."

"Don't say that," he says. "Let's get some coffee and some rest. Everything will be better after some rest." He pulls me against him, and I lean my head against his chest. I breathe in his earthy scent. I love him. I have always loved him and I probably always will. And that is why I must do the right thing. I push hard against him.

"No. You have to leave me. You can't save me," I cry. "You couldn't then, and you can't now." His expression falls from hope and sympathy to anguish. I can't stand to be the cause of his pain, so I start to walk away from him.

"That's right. Fly away, songbird, just like you always do!" he yells at me, causing me to stop. He comes over to me then and stands in front of me.

I look around the park, grateful it's deserted, so no one except Max is witnessing this.

"You always do this when things get hard. You always run away. Just tell me what happened. Let me in. Please, Bayleigh."

I look into his beautiful eyes, and it breaks my heart to hurt him. "No, you deserve so much better than this." A tear rolls down my hot cheek. "Let me go, Chase."

One thing is for sure—our fling is over before it has ever really started. Which is just as well. I've been kidding myself that it is only about sex, that the heat between me and Chase is all desire and lust. There is too much of the past mixed up in my attraction to him. It would be very easy to let myself start to believe in something that would never be.

He releases his grip and I spin away from him before I can change my mind. I need to get away from him and from this town. Coming here was a huge mistake.

CHAPTER TWENTY-THREE

hase

My head is throbbing on the drive back to the ranch. Emotions are running wild, and I'm torn between wanting to scream at Bayleigh for being so reckless and wanting to hold her and tell her everything will be okay. But honestly, I don't know if it will be. How can I possibly help someone who won't help themselves?

The sting of her words makes my heart ache. There is so much pain still locked up inside her, and I want to help—I'm just not sure how. Now she has locked me out again. Her default when things get bad seems to be running away, and she's doing it again. She's pushing me away once more.

Maybe it's for the best. When she left the first

time, it put my life on an entirely different path. I didn't know what to do without Bayleigh. She had been my reason—my north star. Without her, I was left to forge a life I had never expected to live. The pain of not just losing the woman I loved, but the life we had planned to build together had just about killed me. But I had made peace with it. I had rebuilt my life and found purpose working on the ranch. But then she came back and busted down the walls I'd thought I'd built so strong. She is the only one who can affect me like that, and I want to hate her for it. I hate myself for being so weak where she is concerned. I should have stayed away from her. I knew it would be trouble if I saw her again, but I couldn't help myself. Now I am paying for not trusting my gut and avoiding her.

I park my car outside the main house and head inside. I need to talk to someone about all this and I've always respected my mother's opinion, especially when it comes to Bayleigh.

I open the front door and the smell of pot-roast cooking in the oven greets me. I ground myself in the familiarity and safety of this house. I see my mom come over to greet me as I toe off my boots, and the thought occurs to me how lucky I am to have this. Family. Even if it's just my mom.

Bayleigh has no one. In fact, her mother hates her and blames her for the accident. How must that make her feel? I couldn't even start to imagine.

"Are you okay?" Mom asks me. "You look pale. Come sit down. Dinner's ready to be dished out."

I take my seat at the dining table and watch her in the kitchen, serving the food. "I just saw Bayleigh. She's not doing well."

Mom pauses and looks at me. "It's so horrible what happened to that family," she says. "I always liked Bayleigh, and it was such a tragic accident."

"Apparently she left because her mom told her to," I explain. "Her parents kicked her out because she'd been driving."

My mom sighs. "I knew there must have been a reason she left so suddenly. Especially without telling you."

I put down my fork and lean on my elbows. "If she had come to me first, we could have taken her in, or I could have gone with her. I guess that's the worst part. She just left. Ran away from her problems."

"And it seems like that's what she's done ever since. Numbed herself with drugs and alcohol and whatever else she can find. Poor girl. That accident really turned her life upside down."

"I don't know how to help her. I don't know if anyone can." I sigh. I want to help her. I want that sweet, carefree girl back, but it seems that she is really gone for good and this new Bayleigh is just a shell of the person she used to be.

"She still wears my necklace, you know. That one I

whittled for her." I smile at the memory of finding it hanging safely around her neck.

My mom's eyes widen to the size of saucepans. "The little songbird one? I remember how nervous you were to give her that."

"I was scared she wouldn't like it. But she had me put it on her and she swore she would never take it off. I'm kinda surprised it lasted this long," I admit.

"It's like your love for each other. It survives against all odds." She rests her hand on my arm and squeezes. "Life was never meant to be easy."

I look at my mom's weather-beaten face. She looks older than her sixty years. Farm life is not easy for anyone and my parents have struggled through the bad times like everyone else. Droughts, fire, even tornedos have been challenges that my parents have overcome. Plus the personal struggles. Mom endured three miscarriages, and a stillborn before finally bringing a baby to full term, only to have it die of infant death syndrome two weeks later. The fact that I had come when they had given up all hope seemed a miracle, and they have taught me to appreciate every day and have faith in God and his plans. I'm not the avid church-goer that my mom is. I have my own disagreements with Him and his so-called plans. But I respect my mother's choices.

Her faith helped her immensely when my dad died. She still believes God wants her to keep the farm and not retire to a small house in town. Then again, who would want to buy a desolate, drought-affected farm these days? And even if someone did, the bank would take more from the sale than she would get, no doubt leaving her even worse off. If God has a plan, I sure would like to know what it is.

I hug my mom tightly that night before heading back to my place. Even though I know she wouldn't have stopped me from leaving Sweetgum Valley, having her here was a big reason behind why I didn't move. I've lived here all my life, after all. I know my place in this town. It is safe; it is secure.

Bayleigh's life is anything but. As much as I still have these crazy feelings for her, I am better off without her and all her drama.

I am fine on my own. I have a good life. I don't need more than what I have. Do I?

CHAPTER TWENTY-FOUR

ayleigh

I'VE FUCKED UP.

I know it. Kelly knows it.

"I should tell Brendon," Kelly says as she paces the room. "Especially when I found out there were photos and video of you drinking in the park. But we managed to track down the footage and pay them off before it got leaked to the press."

I have an entire team to clean up my messes. They are good at it too. They cleaned it up all Olivia Pope-style so there is no evidence of the messed up stuff I do.

Their time could be spent so much better.

If photos and video had gotten out, it would have been really, really bad.

"Thank you," I say, but I know the words are not enough. They never are.

I'm still in bed. I came straight back here last night after running from Chase. Max delivered me safely to Kelly, who'd been out of her mind with worry. She had put me to bed where I had cried until I had passed out. My head is throbbing this morning, but I'm grateful for the pain. It reminds me I'm still alive.

"This is the last time I'm covering for you, Bayleigh. You fuck this up again, I'm out." Kelly hands me a fresh bottle of water, which I slug down. I'm so dehydrated.

I feel like shit. Not just physically, with a headache throbbing so hard it hurts to keep my eyes open, but I've hurt people. Kelly and Brendon are counting on me to get this right, and I've let them down. Again.

"I'm sorry." My voice breaks as the tears sting my eyes.

Kelly sits next to me on my bed. She doesn't know about my past or the accident, and in this moment, I really need to talk to someone.

Kelly takes my hand, and I know she will keep this secret stored away with all my other ones. She's bound by an iron-clad NDA, after all, just like Max and everyone else who comes near me.

"Chase and I used to date," I start, but shake my head. "Not just date—we were in love. We'd planned a whole life together. We were going to take our band to Nashville and make it big." I take a breath and Kelly leans forward. "My little sister, Harper, started playing with us too. She was so talented and beautiful. Then one day, we were coming back from a music festival. I was driving, and I got distracted. It was dark, and the road was winding, and I lost control of the car and crashed." I can't hold back the sob that escapes. "Harper was killed."

"Oh, my god." Kelly moves closer and hugs me, her support and warmth cracking into my hard shell.

"My parents blamed me for the crash and kicked me out. I couldn't stay in town after that. It was too much." My voice breaks as I tell her my story. Tears wind down my cheeks, and I remember the pain and anguish on my mother's face when she found out her baby girl had died. Her sweet, innocent daughter. And it was her older daughter's fault.

"I ran away. I didn't even tell Chase I was going because I knew he would try to stop me." I wipe at my eyes. "I knew looking at him would remind me of her, and if I stayed in touch with him, I would never have been able to move on with my life." So I built this half-life instead. Numbing myself from the pain with alcohol, drugs and sex.

"That's why I never wanted to come back here. Seeing this town, Chase. It's all too much. Then I saw my mother, and she still hates me and blames me. She will never get over that."

"I'm so sorry, Bayleigh. That is a horrible thing to have to go through. But it was an accident—it wasn't your fault."

I hear her words but don't bother to tell her that I don't believe her. That I could never forgive myself. I have spent eighteen years living with the guilt and remorse and nothing has ever been able to soothe it.

"Chase found me at the park last night. He saw me and tried to help me, but I pushed him away again. I don't deserve to be loved. I deserve to be punished."

Kelly wipes my tear-stained cheek and looks at me. "You have been in enough support groups and enough therapists' offices to know you need to take it one day at a time. Of course you were triggered by seeing your mother. You slipped up and made a mistake. But this isn't the end. You've gotten sober before; you can do it again. Harper would hate seeing you like this."

I nod and try to refocus. The concert is coming up, and this is still my last chance to redeem myself. Harper would want me to perform. She would want me to live.

"I can fix this," I swear to Kelly. "I can put my life back together."

"I know you can." Kelly smiles at me.

I will do it for Harper.

CHAPTER TWENTY-FIVE

hase

As I make my way towards the hotel entrance, I spot Frankie waving at me from across the street. I wave back and wait for him to catch up as he jogs towards me. I received a message this morning that we will be starting rehearsals after lunch today. Though the text didn't say it explicitly, I have a feeling it's because of what happened yesterday with Bayleigh. She's probably nursing a massive hangover right now. Once again, I consider quitting. But I made a commitment, and I'll stick to it. There's also a chance that her show won't go on now that Bayleigh has had a relapse. I feel terrible; maybe I made the situation worse than it already was. That girl still has a hold on me and drives me insane.

"Hey, I thought I might come watch rehearsal," Frankie says as he catches up to me.

"Did the boss say that was okay?" I ask with a frown. Bayleigh doesn't seem to have any strict rules, but at the same time, I haven't seen anyone but the crew show up before.

"Kelly said it would be okay," he says, and we turn to head inside.

"So, how is it going with the assistant?"

"It's good. I mean, we're keeping it casual, obviously, but that chick is incredible in bed. She's lined up a meeting for me with Bayleigh's manager . . ."

I half listen as Frankie talks. I'm excited for him, but my mind is still full of what went down with Bayleigh yesterday. Just when I thought we had begun something new, she went and did something stupid, like drink. Maybe she has been doing it all the time and I have just been too blind to notice. Maybe she's been lying this whole time. She isn't the same girl I used to know.

We enter the ballroom, and I lead Frankie to where the instruments are set up. I wave a hello to Cassie and the other band members and introduce them to Frankie.

"We hear you're a bit of a rising star," Andy says, and Frankie grins proudly.

"That's the plan," he replies.

Cassie hands him a mic. "Show us then. We're a pretty good judge of talent."

Frankie chuckles and throws me a glance. I nod encouragingly and he takes the mic. Frankie is a natural-born performer, and he's always ready to give it his all. He starts singing his favorite cover of a popular country song and before he gets too far in, the rest of the band joins in. I pull on my guitar and strum along, too.

I know our band sounds good when we play at Monty's, and I can't tell if it's these top of the line instruments or the talent playing them, but this song sounds the best it ever has. I can tell from the look on Frankie's face that he's thinking the same thing.

I'm so carried away in the music that I almost miss the side door opening. But, like a sixth sense, I know the second Bayleigh lays eyes on me.

She looks tired. Like, truly exhausted, down to the bone. It must have been a rough night.

Frankie stops singing abruptly when he sees her and slips the mic back in the stand. "I'm sorry, Ms. Gilmore. The band said I could."

Bayleigh walks over to him with a soft smile. "It's okay, Frankie. It's nice to see how passionate you are about your music."

Kelly stands next to her and grins. "Maybe you should hire him for the band."

Bayleigh looks from Frankie to Kelly with a knowing look. "No, he's destined for more than a backup singer."

She smiles at him again before ushering Cassie

over, and I watch the two of them have a private conversation. Bayleigh hands Cassie her phone, and Cassie reads something on the screen. Then Bayleigh looks over at me and our gazes meet. I can't tear my eyes away from her. I desperately want to apologize to her, to make things okay between us again. She'll be gone after the show tomorrow night, and I can't let her leave like this.

She turns back to Cassie and pockets her phone, and turns to me. I drink her in dressed in her tight denim jeans, floral shirt, and dark brown cowgirl boots.

A strand of her curly blonde hair falls on her face, and my hand itches to brush it away for her.

"Chase, I . . ." She swallows before continuing. "I'm sorry about last night. I was having a really bad day. I never should have involved you."

I take a step closer to her so we aren't overheard. "I'm sorry too. I reacted badly. Can we talk?"

She looks at the crew standing around, waiting. "After rehearsal?"

I nod and she offers me a tight smile before taking her position in front of everyone and speaking loudly. "I want to add a new song to the setlist, if that's okay with everyone."

My eyes widen, and I hear murmurs of surprise from the others.

"I know it's last minute, but I only need one accompaniment." She looks at me. "Chase? You already know some of it."

I tilt my head. Does she mean Harper's song?

She nods as though reading my mind. "Do you remember the music?"

It is a tune I will never forget, no matter how hard I might try. Even though we haven't finished it, I can follow her lead and improvise. It's how we work best, after all.

With the guitar still in my hands, I join her at the front of the stage. "Let's do it."

I strum a chord on my guitar, and Bayleigh positions herself in front of the microphone. Her voice shakes with emotion as she sings the first words of the song. The melody is slow and simple, allowing her powerful lyrics and vocal range to take center stage.

I can't tear my eyes away from Bayleigh as she pours her heart out through her singing. The song takes me on a journey of love and loss, heartbreak and surrender. She has added new parts that are vulnerable and raw, and I can feel the healing in her voice. This is no longer just Harper's song; it's transcended into something greater, as if Harper herself is there with us.

It is the most powerful song I have ever heard. When Bayleigh hits the final note, I release a trembling breath, completely moved by her performance.

Silence falls around us, and she looks over at me with a questioning raise of her eyebrows.

"That was amazing," I say quietly, so only she can hear.

That's when the applause breaks out behind us. Kelly rushes over and hugs Bayleigh first and then me. "I knew you could do it."

"We did it." Bayleigh reaches for my hand and I take it in mine.

"And Harper. We all did it," I say, and I watch as a single tear slides down Bayleigh's cheek.

CHAPTER TWENTY-SIX

ayleigh

Everyone's riding high afterwards. Especially me. Writing and performing that song has done more to heal my heart than years of therapy ever could.

We run through the set one more time and go over the last-minute details. Tomorrow morning, we will be going to the outdoor stage for sound check then to the big show. I'm nervous and excited and scared, but knowing Chase will be beside me makes me surprisingly less anxious. He has a strange, calming effect that I'd forgotten about.

I tell Kelly and Max I'm going to hang out with Chase. "I'll call if I need you," I say. "We'll be fine."

"Okay then. Call if you need anything," Kelly says,

then I watch as she wanders over to Frankie, who sat watching our entire rehearsal. It's their last night together, too, and I'm glad they will be able to spend it together uninterrupted.

Max gives me a stern look. "Don't do anything stupid."

"I won't. Enjoy your night off," I tell him. I walk over to find Chase putting his guitar in its case, and I reach over to touch his arm. He's wearing a plaid blue and white shirt, and it brings out the blue of his eyes. He smells deliciously woody, and I want to snuggle into him.

But I resist the urge. We have a lot to talk about, and he deserves to know a few things.

"Hey." He straightens and gazes at me. I could lose myself in that gaze. What would it be like to see it every day?

"Can we go somewhere?" I ask. My hand is still on his arm, and I'm not in any hurry to drop it.

"Sure. Where do you wanna go?"

"You'll see."

He squints at me before slinging his guitar over his shoulder and following me out. We chat about the show as he leads me to his car and opens the passenger door for me. I slide in and wait as he places his instrument in the backseat and settles in behind the steering wheel.

"Now where?" he asks.

I suck in a breath before asking, "Can you please take me to Harper's grave?"

He nods and starts the car without question. That's one of the things I love about him. He knows when to ask questions, and when not to.

The drive is a short one through residential streets and we pull up at the entrance to the cemetery at dusk. I climb out of the car and look around. The last time I was here, I was at my sister's funeral. I don't remember much about it. I was still in shock and deep in grief.

Chase comes to stand next to me, and I look up at him. "I don't know where she is."

"I do." He reaches his hand to the small of my back. "I'll take you there."

We walk quietly through the rows of gravestones, his hand remaining in place. I take in the flower bouquets and gifts left on the majority of newer graves as we pass. It is a peaceful spot, surrounded by trees and flowering bushes.

Chase stops and points to a simple grass plot with a stone headstone. A fresh bouquet of colorful flowers sits in a jar next to it.

I walk closer and feel Chase's hand slip away. I'm grateful for the moment alone he is giving me to be with my sister.

I sit on my knees on the grass covering her and read the gravestone.

Harper Elizabeth Gilmore
Beloved daughter and sister

Forever singing in the angel choir.

I can't hold back the tears any longer, and they flow quietly down my cheeks. Memories of Harper flow through my mind like a disjointed movie as I let her in. I run my hand over the smooth marble and the inscription—so simple and yet so perfect. She will be singing with the angels—there is no doubt in my mind. Her voice was God-given and so has been returned.

"Hi sis," I whisper down at the grass in front of me. "I'm sorry I didn't come sooner. I bet you know everything that's happened in the last eighteen years. It's been quite the journey here without you." I glance at the flowers again. They look fresh, and the gravestone is well maintained. I wonder how often my mother comes here. Daily perhaps? Prolonging her grief and misery, when that isn't what Harper would have wanted. What she's doing isn't healthy—but it's nothing in comparison to the way I've ruined my life.

"You would hate me for all the mistakes and bad choices I've made. They just seemed to snowball. And the more mistakes I made, the more I needed to drown the pain in drugs and alcohol. I needed to numb myself from it. I know that now and I won't do it anymore." I sniff through my tears. "I promise you, Harper, I will make you proud of me. I will bring our song to the world and share it the way we would have shared it together. I have so many other ideas now, and I know you have a hand in that."

"She will always be with you, Bayleigh. Love like that never dies," Chase says from behind me.

I look up at him. "No, it doesn't." My love for him is still there, stronger than ever in this moment when the three of us are together in the only way we can be now. "We were with her at the end, and she will be with us at our end."

"Which will not be for a very, very long time." He kneels down beside me and strokes his hand down my cheek, wiping my tears away.

"It was my fault," I whisper. "I should have been concentrating more." Fresh tears sting my eyes, and he gathers me against him.

"It was an accident. A terrible, tragic accident." He tangles his fingers in my hair and kisses the top of my head.

"I was responsible for her. I was the driver."

"She wasn't wearing a seatbelt. I should have stopped her from distracting you. We all could have done things differently." He says the words all my therapists have told me over the years, but they make sense coming from him. "We can't change the past as much as we want to."

Silently, I think about my other mistakes and things I have done. Would he still want me if he knew all I'd done? There is still so much I've kept secret. Things the press has never found out beyond just what happened with my sister. Regrets that haunt me still. I can never tell him. He can never find out.

We sit there for a long time, comforting each other the way we should have been in the weeks after the accident.

"I miss her so much," I whisper.

"I know you do. So do I. She would want you to be happy, Bayleigh. She would be so proud of your success."

"I just couldn't stay here without her. She was everywhere." My voice wavers.

He exhales loudly. "You should have come to me. I would have looked after you."

"I know," I whisper. "But I was so ashamed. I didn't want to ruin your life, too."

"You wouldn't have ruined it. We were always better together," he says.

He's right. We were better together. We were a team and still could be. We belong together. We always have. I have loved him my entire life. He has always been my best friend. My soulmate. The only one for me. I carry secrets he can never know about, but I want him, need him so much right now. All my worries, all my doubts, all the pressures and uncertainties will still be there tomorrow. Right now, in Chase's arms, I have everything I need.

He is an admirable man. Sexy, strong, determined. The kind of man a woman could build a life with. I raise my hand and thread my fingers through the thick hair behind his ear and gently, slowly tug his head towards me. He stares deep into my eyes and whispers my name as a question.

"Please?" I whisper back, and a second later, his lips are on mine. My lips part on a soft sigh and my arms encircle his neck. As he angles his head to deepen our kiss, I press myself closer. When we break apart and stare at each other, both of our breathing is uneven. His arms enfold me, anchoring me against him, his hand warm on the bare skin of my shoulder.

"Take me home?" I ask him.

"To my place?" he asks, and I nod. I want to see how he lives. Who he is in the real world and not just the cocoon this week has provided us with.

He helps me up and we walk back to his car. The evening is very quiet, the moon no more than a ghostly shimmer behind the clouds, and an owl hoots somewhere in the distance. I take a deep breath of the cool and clear night air. I savor the feeling of peace and safety, as though simply being with Chase is enough to keep the pain away. If only it could always be like this. It's a silly thought, and I don't want to dwell on what tomorrow will bring. For right now, this is enough. One more night will be enough.

CHAPTER TWENTY-SEVEN

hase

THE SUN DIPS low on the horizon, painting the sky in a breathtaking array of oranges and pinks that reflect off the weathered fence posts lining the dusty road. As we pull up to the ranch, the familiar sight of the old red barn and sprawling pastures greets us, bathed in the warm glow of twilight. The horses, mere silhouettes, graze peacefully in the distance, their gentle movements a stark contrast to the tumultuous emotions I can sense radiating from Bayleigh.

I guide the truck down the winding path that leads to my cottage, set apart from the main house and nestled among a stand of sweetgum trees. Their leaves rustle softly in the evening breeze, whispering secrets of days long past. The cottage comes into view and I park in front.

"I built this place to give my parents some privacy," I say as I fumble with my seatbelt.

"Privacy for them or you?" She raises an eyebrow at me, which I ignore, and I climb out of the vehicle.

She follows me inside and I pause to turn on the light. She walks into the room and looks around at the sparse furniture. "It's cozy."

She takes off her denim jacket and drapes it over the couch. I take a moment to observe the smudges beneath her eyes. I know she needs comfort, and I want to be there for her. Without hesitation, I stride over to her, and she settles into me as I wrap my arms around her back. Her head rests against my chest, and I inhale the sweet scent of her perfume. Having her close feels so right—like we're finally whole again. Without her, something is always missing.

Her head tilts, her lips searching for mine and we kiss, softly this time.

Our kiss deepens as passion ignites between us. My hands roam over Bayleigh's back, pulling her closer as she threads her fingers through my hair.

As our lips part, Bayleigh's eyes meet mine, shimmering with emotion in the dim light. Her fingers trace along my jawline, sending shivers down my spine.

"Chase," she whispers, her voice barely audible. "I'm so sorry. For everything."

I pull her closer, feeling her body tremble slightly

against mine. "Shh, it's okay," I murmur into her hair. "You're here now. That's what matters."

She looks up at me, vulnerability etched across her face. "But I hurt you. I left without a word. I pushed you away for so long."

"We were both hurting," I say softly. "What happened to Harper . . . it broke all of us. You did what you had to do to survive."

A tear slips down her cheek, and I gently brush it away with my thumb.

Bayleigh's eyes glisten with unshed tears as she looks up at me. "I don't deserve your forgiveness, Chase. I've made so many mistakes."

I cup her face gently in my hands. "We all make mistakes, Bay. What matters is that you're here now, trying to make things right."

She leans into my touch, her eyes closing briefly. When she opens them again, the vulnerability there takes my breath away. "I've missed you so much," she whispers. "All these years, no matter who I was with or what I was doing, a part of me was always missing. *You* were missing."

My heart swells at her words. I've felt the exact same way, like a piece of me left with her all those years ago. Having her here in my arms feels like coming home.

She slowly removes her clothes. Making a sport of it as she watches me watch her. When she's finished undressing, I guide her backwards, my hands supporting her as I lift her onto the dining table. With anticipation shining in her eyes, she willingly spreads her legs for me as I position myself between them. My eager hands quickly remove her bra, allowing me to take in the sight of her exposed breasts. As I lean in closer, my hands gently caress her inner thighs, and shivers race over her body. Our lips meet with an intense and urgent hunger, and I'm no longer concerned with being gentle or sweet. We press our bodies together, and I need more than just kisses.

I explore Bayleigh's curves with my hands, reacquainting myself with every dip and curve of her body. She arches into my touch, soft moans escaping her lips as I massage her breasts. Her nipples harden under my touch, and I lower my head to suck on one while swirling my tongue around it.

Her fingers tangle in my hair as I lavish attention on her breasts. Her hips move against mine, as if they're seeking friction. I slide a hand between her thighs and can feel the heat radiating from her core, even through the fabric of her jeans. When I press against her center, she lets out a whimper and throws her head back in pleasure.

I free myself from my jeans, desperate to be inside of her. She lays back on the table and opens herself to me. I guide my erection between her thighs and let out a low groan as the tightness of her heat envelopes me.

Then I am sliding into her depths, slow and long in exactly the way I know she likes it. I stroke into her once, twice, feeling her body arch as she pants beneath me. With each thrust, my cock strums her, teasing and taunting her slick folds until she can't take it anymore.

I savor the feeling of her silky heat enveloping me as I drive into her over and over. Her legs wrap tightly around my waist, pulling me even closer as our hips move in a frenzied rhythm.

"Chase," she gasps, her nails digging into my shoulders. "Oh God, yes!"

Her inner walls start to quiver and clench around me. Wanting to push her over the edge, I slide a hand between our bodies to rub tight circles on her sensitive bundle of nerves. Her reaction is instant—her back bows and a cry of pleasure escapes her lips.

"That's it, baby," I encourage, increasing the pressure and speed of my fingers. "Let go for me."

Her entire body tenses as waves of ecstasy crash over her. She clamps down on me as she climaxes, her face contorting in pleasure. The sight and sensation of her orgasm quickly pushes me over the edge as well. With a few final deep thrusts, I bury myself inside her and find my own release.

We cling to each other as the aftershocks roll through us, our breathing ragged and bodies slick with sweat. I pepper soft kisses along her neck and shoulder as we slowly come down from our high.

I carefully withdraw from her and help her off the table. Her legs are a bit shaky, so I scoop her up in my arms and carry her to the bathroom. "I'm going to run us a bath," I say as I put her on her feet and turn on the tap of the large bathtub.

Bayleigh leans against the bathroom counter, watching as I adjust the water temperature and add some lavender-scented bubble bath. The sweet aroma fills the small space as steam begins to rise from the tub.

I turn to her, taking in her tousled hair and flushed cheeks. Even after all these years, she is still the most beautiful woman I've ever seen. I close the distance between us and cup her face gently in my hands.

"You're so beautiful," I murmur, brushing my lips softly against hers.

She smiles up at me, a hint of vulnerability in her eyes. "So are you."

I help her into the tub before climbing in behind her. She settles back against my chest with a contented sigh as the warm water laps over us. For a long moment, we just sit in comfortable silence, enjoying the closeness. We soak for nearly an hour, washing each other's backs, talking about the concert, the business, my art. Afterward, I towel her dry and dress her.

"I should probably head back to the hotel," she responds when I ask if she wants to spend the night. "Tomorrow is a big day."

How could I forget? After tomorrow, there will be no reason for her to stay with me. But I push away that thought and focus on enjoying our time together now. I give her one last kiss, trying to memorize every detail. Who knows how many more of these moments we will have? "I'll drive you back to town."

CHAPTER TWENTY-EIGHT

ayleigh

As Chase pulls up in front of the hotel, I feel a pang of longing. I don't want this night to end. His hand rests on my thigh, warm and comforting.

"I'll see you tomorrow," he says softly.

I nod, not trusting my voice. After a moment's hesitation, I lean over and kiss him deeply, trying to convey everything I can't say out loud. When we finally break apart, both slightly breathless, I whisper a quiet "thank you" before slipping out of the truck.

I watch him drive away, the taillights fading into the darkness, before heading inside. The lobby is quiet at this late hour, just a lone night clerk behind the desk who nods politely as I pass.

In the elevator, I lean against the wall and close my eyes, replaying the events of the evening in my mind. The raw emotion at Harper's grave, the tenderness and passion with Chase at his cottage . . . For the first time in years, I feel a glimmer of hope. Maybe I can find a way to heal, to move forward without completely abandoning my past.

The elevator dings and I make my way down the hall to my room. As I fumble for my key card, the door next to mine opens and Kelly steps out, looking disheveled.

"There you are!" she exclaims. "I was starting to worry."

I give her a small smile. "I'm fine. Just . . . had some things to take care of."

Kelly's eyes narrows as she takes in my appearance —slightly damp hair, flushed cheeks. A knowing smirk spreads across her face.

"Things, huh? Would those things happen to involve a certain handsome guitar player?"

My cheeks flush even more under Kelly's scrutiny. "Maybe," I admit with a small smile.

Kelly's eyes light up. "Ooh, details please! Was it good? I bet it was good."

I laugh and shake my head. "A lady doesn't kiss and tell." But I can't quite hide my satisfied grin.

"Fine, keep your secrets," Kelly says with a dramatic sigh. "But seriously, are you okay? After yesterday . . ."

The reminder of my breakdown sobers me quickly.

"I'm . . . better," I say carefully. "Chase and I talked. About a lot of things. It helped."

Kelly nods, her expression turning serious. "I'm glad. You know I'm here if you need anything, right?"

"I know," I say softly, touched by her concern. "Thank you, Kelly. For everything."

Her grin grows wider as she leans in to share her news. "Brendon called today. They want you to perform at a show in Nashville next weekend. And it's not just any show."

My eyes widen in surprise as she names the venue, which can hold up to a thousand people. It may not be the biggest audience I've ever played to, but it's definitely a step in the right direction.

"That's amazing!" My heart is beating fast with excitement. Offers are already coming in before the show tomorrow night. This could be the turning point I've been waiting for. Even if it means leaving Chase behind. We both knew this was only temporary—just for old times' sake.

The thought of leaving him and never seeing him again fills me with dread. I can't bear the idea of walking away from the relationship, but I also can't give up on my own dreams and ambitions. If only he would be willing to leave everything behind and join me on this crazy journey. Perhaps he would. A glimmer of hope sparks within me, and I hold onto it tightly. It is the only way we could make things work. If he truly cares about me as much as I do about him, maybe he will take a chance and start a new life with me.

Later, when I'm in bed as I drift off to sleep, I fantasize about all the possibilities our future could hold together.

Him performing on stage with me, playing, loving, sharing our lives together just as we always should have been.

CHAPTER TWENTY-NINE

hase

I WAKE up and take a moment to clear my head. Did last night really happen with Bayleigh, or was it just a dream? The smell of her on my sheets confirms that it was real. I've dreamed about her for years, her scent, her taste. But being with her in real life is so much better. She's like a drug, addictive and irresistible. No matter what drama she puts me through, I am always there, begging for more.

As I think back on our passionate night together, a grin spreads across my face. Her body against mine, the way she cried out my name—I want more of it all. I want her every night in my bed, and to wake up with her in my arms every morning.

I know it's not healthy how consumed I am by her. But I can't help it. I've spent so long pining for her, waiting for her to come back and give my life purpose again.

I rub my hand over my face, thinking about how pathetic it all sounds. But she has this power over me that I can't break, no matter how hard I try. And trust me—I've tried.

My eyes drift to the watch on my bedside table. Today is the big day—the day that will make or break Bayleigh's career. If she succeeds, she'll get to go back to touring, making music, and living the life of fame and fortune.

But if she doesn't . . . I don't even want to think about it. It's too painful to imagine a future without her in it.

I can't help but ponder if life will be simpler for us if she doesn't achieve her dreams. Maybe then she'll come back and we could have a real chance of being together. She could move in with us at the ranch and lend a hand. Perhaps she could even teach music at the local school. We could finally have the family we've always dreamed of. We aren't too old for that, are we? But deep down, I know it isn't just about moving away from Nashville's hustle and bustle to the slower pace of Sweetgum Valley. If that had been enough for her, she wouldn't have left. And if I had been enough, we would have found a way to make it work together.

But I promised to support her, and that's exactly

what I'll do. Whether or not tonight is a success, I won't let it fail because of me. All I want is for her to be happy, and if this is what she wants, then that's all that matters.

Being near her this week has been bittersweet. It's only intensified my desire for her.

As I shower and dress, I resign myself to be happy with the time we've had together. It was more than I ever expected, and I will take these memories with me forever. This brief happiness will be worth every shred of pain that I will no doubt feel when she leaves.

I head to the main house for breakfast with my mom. She has bacon sizzling when I get there, and I give her cheek a kiss as I reach for the coffee.

Today's the day. Are you excited?" she asks me.

"Yeah. We have a media junket this morning, then sound check before the big show." I wonder if I'll get to talk to Bayleigh alone today. It is a busy day, and she has a lot to do to get ready. I don't want to distract her, but I do want to get a chance to wish her luck.

"I'm so excited to watch you perform tonight," Mom continues, handing me a plate of eggs and bacon.

"You've seen me play at Monty's. This will just be on a bigger scale." A much bigger scale, with an outdoor stage, proper lighting, and sound.

"And it's getting streamed live. Maybe you'll get offered a deal like Frankie."

I chuckle. "I doubt it. I'm only on guitar. No one

will even notice me. Not when they can be looking at Bayleigh."

Mom looks at me then, studying me like she can see all my secrets. "You want to be with her."

I stop chewing, and my mind races. Can she read my thoughts? "It's not like that. Besides, she's only here for the show," I say defensively.

"I remember how close you two were as kids. When she left, it was like a piece of you went with her," my mom says softly, her understanding eyes trained on me.

My heart clenches at the mention of Bayleigh and how Mom was there for me during the most difficult time of my life after the accident. Bayleigh had no one to lean on. She was young and all alone when she left.

"It was hard then, and it will be hard when she leaves again. But what other choice do we have? How can a bird and a fish make it work?" I sigh, staring down at my plate.

"There's a piece of you that belongs to her, and she'll take it with her when she leaves," my mom says gently, placing a comforting hand over mine.

Her words hit me hard. I could go with Bayleigh, but what about my obligations to this ranch? My mom interrupts my thoughts with a suggestion that catches me off guard—"We could sell the ranch and start fresh somewhere else."

I look at her with wide eyes. "No, we can't do that."

She shrugs. "Why not? This was your father's dream. It's not yours though."

"But this place is everything to you. It's Dad's legacy." I interject.

"It's not the same without him here." Her voice fades off and I look around the kitchen where so many family meals have taken place. I am filled with memories—both good and bad. I couldn't just give it up. Could I?

This is my home, my safe haven. I don't think I could ever leave it behind. But maybe . . . just maybe . . . it's worth considering.

Would being with Bayleigh be worth it, if it meant sacrificing my own desires? I have no idea what she wants or if there is even a place for me in her life. She is constantly on the go and has little time to think about the future. I can't help but wonder if she would even have space for me in her busy life. But despite these doubts, a glimmer of hope remains as I finish my breakfast and make my way into town. It is a hope that I've never allowed myself to entertain before, but now it lingers, begging to be explored.

ayleigh

THE MORNING PASSES QUICKLY, consumed by phone calls, meetings, and preparations for tonight's show. I hardly have a moment to think about Chase and the night we shared.

"We have this media junket first, then soundcheck, and finally we can get you into hair and makeup," Kelly says as she guides me through the hotel to another room where members of the press are waiting. I see Chase, Cassie, and the others standing in front of a closed door. Our eyes meet, and I can't help but smile at him.

He's dressed in a blue denim shirt that makes him look like he just walked off the ranch. He looks sexy as hell, and I know the female audience will go wild for this cowboy. A pang of jealousy hits me. I don't want those women lusting after him, undressing him with their eyes. He belongs to me and only to me.

Well, damn. That definitely complicates things. But I push the thought aside. I don't have time for these emotions right now. My focus needs to be on my job, and dealing with the media is a big part of that. We have to put on a good show here before we even step foot on stage.

"Good luck, everyone!" Kelly shouts out before opening the door for us to enter. Cassie goes in first, followed by myself, and then the others take their seats on the stage.

I look out at the audience. The room is full of people. From the local newspaper to social media influencers and tabloid reporters. I hate them the most and my eyes stop when I see Laura Evens sitting in the front row. I swear that woman has it out for me. Her life mission seems to be to reveal all my secrets. She's cracked a few, but thankfully not the biggest. That could be the final nail on the coffin of my career, and I send up a quick prayer that she will stay far away from finding out the truth.

"Bayleigh, how does it feel to be back home?" a man in the second row asks.

I put on a smile and speak into the microphone in front of me. "It's been wonderful being back and connecting with friends and seeing how much the community has grown and how they are coming together in this time of need." I recite the words Kelly and I practiced.

"Chase, have you ever performed on a stage like this before?" someone else asks, turning their attention to the man in the denim shirt. He appears calm and collected, although I know he hates being singled out. He always used to prefer sharing the spotlight with me. And if I'm honest, I prefer that too.

"No, not this big. But I've been told it's going to be an incredible show, and I hope we can raise a substantial amount of money to assist struggling ranchers and farmers," he responds with a grin. He's a natural at this.

"Is it true that you and Bayleigh used to be in a relationship when you both lived here?"

I recognize Laura's high-pitched voice, and I narrow my eyes at her and think of an answer.

But Chase gets in first "We grew up together and were good friends."

Laura presses for more information. "Just good friends?"

I interrupt before Chase can say anything that would raise more questions. "Yes, we were close friends in the past, and it's been great catching up. Plus, I'm excited to showcase some of the talented musicians from Sweetgum Valley. Chase performs most Saturday nights with Frankie Calhoun at Monty's. You should come see him perform; he's going to be a big name in country music."

I turn to look at Chase and smile, noticing the admiration in his eyes.

"Any other questions about the concert?" I ask the audience, redirecting their attention back to the event and its purpose: raising funds for our community. This event is about more than just my career; it's about giving back to the place that shaped me and the people who will always hold a special place in my heart. From then on, all questions revolve around the show and our fundraising efforts, which I am grateful for.

Once the interview is finished, we make our way to the driveway, where a group of fans are waiting for us. They wave and call out my name as we duck into the awaiting cars. The ride to the stadium is short, and I immediately recognize it as the old rodeo grounds. It is now filled with portable buildings and scaffolding for the stage.

"We have trailers set up for you to get ready in after soundcheck," Kelly points out as we walk backstage, passing by the crew who are putting the finishing touches on the setup. I step onto the stage and walk towards the center, where my microphone is already set up. In front of me are rows of folding chairs, while in the distance there are bleachers for people to sit on. It isn't a massive venue, but it is still sizeable for a small town like this one.

Chase joins me at my side. "It's all sold out," he says, gesturing to the arena around us. "Everyone wants to be here and support you."

I turn to face him, wanting to reach out and hold him close, but aware of the others waiting behind us.

"Once the lights are on, it'll be hard to see the audience tonight," I say. "I always like to come out before and see it empty like this. So many performers never make it this far."

"You earned it. You worked hard for this moment. You've been through a lot," he replies, his hand brushing against mine.

I turn towards him fully, feeling overwhelmed by emotion. "It should have been us. Together from the beginning. I'm sorry I took that away from you."

"I understand why you did what you did. It's all in the past now," Chase says reassuringly.

I look into his eyes and take a deep breath. "I've already been offered a show in Nashville. And I want you to perform with me. I want you by my side."

Chase's Adam's apple bobs as he swallows, and I stare at the shadowy stubble on his jawline.

"I don't know what to say," he whispers.

I reach up and brush my fingers against his stubbly cheek, reveling in the sensation of the bristles against my skin. "Just say you'll think about it. This doesn't have to end."

He meets my gaze and nods. "I'll think about it."

A surge of hope fills my heart—there is nothing more I want than for him to be by my side. He tucks a loose strand of hair behind my ear, his touch gentle and caring.

"The way you touch me . . . it means everything," I whisper, feeling vulnerable and exposed. Knowing that he not only understands my pain but also wants to hold me through it fills me with gratitude and love. I am in love with this man—his very presence sets my soul on fire. He's everything I never thought I'd have again.

"Bayleigh, everyone's ready," Kelly calls out, and I can hear the amusement in her voice.

I clear my thoughts and spin around. "Alright, where's my earpiece? Let's do this."

After finishing our sound check, we retreat to our trailers to get ready for the show. I carefully select my outfit, settling on the white dress and belt that Kelly and I picked out while shopping together. My cowgirl boots have intricate patterns of pink and blue flowers and are designed for comfort. The stylist works her magic on my curly hair, and I can hardly recognize myself once she's finished with my makeup.

There is a knock at the door and my heart leaps with anticipation, hoping it's Chase. But when Matthew Butler pokes his head in, I force a friendly smile despite feeling disappointed.

He's undeniably handsome, with thick brown hair and piercing blue eyes. He's the epitome of the new generation of country music and has a fan base that reaches beyond the genre. But I can't bring myself to hate him for it. Maybe envy him a little, but not hate. I understand what it takes to make it in this industry, and I know he must have faced challenges and struggles as well.

"I just wanted to wish you luck for tonight," he says, grasping my hand. "You've done such a great job promoting this town; I wish I had time to see it."

"Thanks," I reply. "It was a wonderful place to grow up in."

"I heard about your Nashville gig—congratulations! You'll be touring again soon enough."

I return his smile. "Thank you for the encouragement. And best of luck to you as well in your future endeavors."

"Thanks. That means a lot coming from you. Have a good night." He turns and disappears into the darkness.

"It must be almost time," the stylist chimes in as she fusses with my hair again. "You're going to do amazing."

I can't help but smile at her words. "I hope so."

As I prepare to take the stage, it occurs to me that this will be the first time in a long while that I won't need a drink beforehand. The desire for one isn't even present. Tonight, I'll perform sober and clear-headed, doing what I do best: putting on a show.

Nothing fills me with life and energy, like being on stage with the strum of a guitar and the thumping of the bass drum. Music is my therapy, my outlet, and I am ready to pour my heart into every note.

Kelly rounds us up backstage when it's time, and we all form a circle. Each of us takes a deep breath, and I mentally prepare myself for the next few hours, where I'll push my body to the limit. As I look at each member of our group, I know they will give their all tonight. From here, I can hear the audience buzzing with excitement and anticipation as the emcee hypes them up for our entrance. After our performance, Matthew will take the stage, but even if only half of the crowd came to see us specifically, we're determined to leave a lasting impression.

"I'm so grateful to all of you," I say, making eye contact with everyone. "I couldn't do this without you." My eyes land on Chase and he winks at me, causing my stomach to flip-flop.

"Have a good show," Kelly says a second after we are announced, and she waves us up the stairs.

The band file ahead. and I find Chase and touch his arm. When he pauses to turn to me, I raise up on my tiptoes and kiss his lips. "This is how it's supposed to be," I whisper into his ear. He presses another kiss to my lips and leads me out.

The crowd roars as I walk across the stage, waving and taking it all in. Lights flash in front of me. People yell out and clap. I get to the center and take the silver mic from the stand and raise a hand. "Thank y'all for being here!" I look out as far as I can see into the darkness where I know the bleachers are. "We're here for a cause which is close to my heart, and that is to raise money for drought relief here in Sweetgum Valley. Who wants to raise some money?"

As the applause and cheers continue, I can't help but marvel at how loud the noise is in this small venue. "You guys are amazing! Your energy is infectious!"

I strut around the stage, making eye contact with members of the audience in the front row. I want each and every one of them to know that I see them and appreciate their support.

"It's been a while since I've performed, but I'm back now and ready to give it my all tonight. And so is my band." I introduce them one by one. "And many of you may already know Chase Tutton on guitar, our newest member. We're thrilled to have him join us for this show."

Someone in the crowd hoots and calls out, "Yeah, Chase!"

Then, I signal to Cassie to count us in, and the crowd roars as we start our set with my most famous song.

Being on stage feels like home; music is where I come alive. And judging by the way the audience is singing along and dancing, they feel it too. Each song we play has a different tone—some are about forgiveness, others about finding inner peace, and of course there are plenty about love. With every note and lyric, I pour my heart into the performance, losing myself in the music. This is where I belong, under the spotlight, sharing my passion with the world. There's no doubt in my mind that this is where I'm meant to be.

When we get to our song, I look at Chase and he

joins me at the front of the stage. The lights shine brightly on us. The crowd is quiet with anticipation.

I lower my mic and look at him. "Are you ready?"

He looks at me with a smile. "Are you?"

I nod and watch as he sets the guitar low on his hip and begins to play, strumming each individual chord over and over again. I keep my eye on the crowd, encouraging him to continue to play while I prepare them.

"This is a new song," I address the audience. "I started writing it many years ago when I lived here, and with Chase's help, I finally finished it this week. It's a very special song that means a lot to both of us." I lower the mic and glance up at the dark sky above us. "Harper, this is for you." I whisper into the night.

Closing my eyes, I can feel her presence beside us as Chase's chords blend seamlessly with my voice. The lyrics flow from me effortlessly, almost as if they'd been ingrained in my mind all along. As I sing, I envision my sweet, innocent, beautiful little sister standing onstage beside us, just like she had been when we performed at our last show together.

Every chord Chase plays and every breath I take, it feels like Harper is right here with us. A tear runs down my cheek, but I embrace the emotion and pour it into the music.

I unleash all the feelings I've held back for years and channel them into my performance. I hold the last note and let it linger. Then there's a brief moment of silence before the audience erupts in applause, snapping me back to reality. I jump slightly when Chase places his hand on my back, but then I melt into his touch as I see every emotion I feel mirrored in his eyes. Without hesitation, I wrap my arms around him and hold on tight. In that moment, I know he is my anchor, my safe haven, my rock. As much as I need to spread my wings and fly, I also need a place to come back to when I get tired. He is that place for me—my home, my love.

* * *

"THAT WAS INCREDIBLE! You killed it tonight!" Kelly exclaims, giving me a tight hug as I step off the stage. We didn't even bother finishing the last two songs in our set—nothing could top the standing ovation we received after our duet.

"That was the best performance of your career!" Kelly continues. "People may have come to see Matthew Butler, but they'll never forget you."

It's hard to gauge the size of the audience when you're on stage with bright lights shining in your eyes, but the energy and noise were unlike they've been at any other show I've played. Everyone was captivated by our performance, and I could hear many people singing along to our duet even though it was the first time we'd played it. It's beyond anything I ever imagined, to have a crowd singing words that I wrote.

Our voices intertwined perfectly, reaching deep

into my soul. This is what I've been missing all this time. Chase has filled a void that I'd thought would be empty forever.

I take a deep breath, trying to ground myself and savor this high from such an amazing performance.

"Way to go, Bayleigh. I knew you could do it!" Matthew says with a grin as he passes me on his way to the stage. I smile broadly. This night couldn't get any better, and I want to remember every precious moment of it.

Chase spots me in the midst of the crowd and comes over to me, lifting me up by my waist and twirling me around as I laugh with joy. His embrace is so comforting, making me never want to let go. When he sets me down, I wrap my arms around his neck and press my lips against his warm skin.

"That was beyond amazing," I gush.

"It was more than I could have ever imagined," he whispers, and kisses the tip of my nose sweetly.

"And you are even more than I could have ever dreamed of," I reply, standing on my tiptoes to give him a kiss. I don't care if anyone sees us or if my lipstick smudges; I just need him to know how much I love him and want him in my life, even if I can't say it out loud.

He pulls back from the kiss and nuzzles his face against my ear. "I love you, Bayleigh. And I really want to make this work between us."

His words fill my heart with happiness, but I need

to make sure we're on the same page. "But what about Nashville?"

"I'll come out for your show and give it a shot," he promises. "If you want me to."

"Of course I do," I assure him, before sealing our words with another kiss.

"And like they say in AA, let's take it one day at a time," he suggests while brushing away a strand of hair from my face.

"One day at a time," I repeat.

"Let's go. The after-party is waiting." Kelly beckons us to follow her.

She knows better than to schedule one after every show, but for some gigs, it's a necessary part of the job. Especially tonight, when fans and VIPs have paid top dollar to celebrate with us.

Chase holds my hand as we make our way through the bustling corridors. The energy around us is contagious as the band discusses their performance, the highlights, and how the audience responded.

"This is going to open up new opportunities for all of us," Andy remarks, and he's right. Even if they don't stick with me, they could easily join another band after tonight's stellar show. But I hope they'll stay. Having a reliable team is crucial when performing; they enhance my sound and help me deliver the best show possible to the audience.

We enter the room to a thunderous round of applause, and I gasp at the sight of everyone there cheering for us. Kelly stays by my side and guides me towards the VIPs I need to greet. I am grateful for everyone's kind words of encouragement and gratitude.

"I feel bad for Matt, having to follow that performance!" Someone says, and I smile to myself. This night couldn't get any better. I've done what I set out to do—I've proven that I'm not washed up after all, that there are still plenty of miles left in my tank, and I'm going to keep going. This time I'm going to stay focused and sober and with Chase by my side. Who knows how high I can soar?

I hold on to his hand tightly as I feel him slipping away. Our gazes lock, and I am grateful for another chance with him. He is still the same kind and talented man I've known since childhood. Being with him inspires me to be a better person, and I love him for that.

I hear someone calling my name and turn to see a stunning blonde navigating her way through the crowd towards me. Max, who is always on guard, steps in front of her to block her path. But I know everyone has been screened before entering this room, so I place my hand on his shoulder and tell him it's fine. "I'm sure she means no harm."

Her big blue eyes give her an innocent appearance. She's tall and strikingly beautiful with wavy blonde hair—it's like she could be a model.

"Hi, I'm Bayleigh," I say, extending my hand. She

just stares at me, and something about her seems familiar. I furrow my brow, trying to figure out where I've seen her before.

"Are you alright?" Chase's voice breaks through my thoughts, and I turn to see him standing next to me. My heart sinks as I glance from the girl, who couldn't be more than eighteen years old.

My stomach drops as I face the girl once again. Her blue eyes, so familiar to me, meet my gaze without any hesitation. "My name's Chloe," she says, taking a deep breath before delivering the rest of her statement. "I'm your daughter."

Thank you for reading **Songbird**.
Find out what happens next in **Heartbeat Song**.
Buy Now

Bestselling romance author and CEO of Serenade Publishing, Sarah Williams spent her childhood chasing sheep, riding horses and picking Kiwi fruit on the family orchard in rural New Zealand. After a decade travelling, Sarah moved to Queensland, to raise a family and follow her passion for writing. She currently resides on the Sunshine Coast Hinterland, Australia.

Her rural romance series Brigadier Station won the hearts of readers around the world. The audiobooks were narrated by Logie nominated actor Myles Pollard, best known for his role as Nick in *McLeod's Daughters*.

www.sarahwilliamsauthor.com

facebook.com/sarahwilliamswriter

instagram.com/sarahwilliamsauthor

bookbub.com/profile/sarah-williams

goodreads.com/goodreadscomsarahwilliams